"Robbins's melodic novel is a story of war, family, language, but above all, a paean to unabashed, unbridled love. Told in quiet but elegant prose, each thump of this melodic novel's heart (and what an enormous, rousing heart it is) attests to the timeless and life-giving power of love."
—Khaled Hosseini, *New York Times*–bestselling author of *The Kite Runner*

"A stunning first novel on love, loss and language." —*The Chicago Tribune*

"A beautifully crafted story . . . Her poetic style plunges the reader into the scene, her tone reminiscent of Camus. . . . *A Word for Love* made *this* reader cry from feeling the transformative, redemptive power of fiction. This profoundly satisfying novel ventures to the very heart of romance and its literary origins in the seventh-century lyric poetry of the Arabian desert."
—*Washington Independent Review of Books*

"Emily Robbins has written a lyrical story about love in nearly all of its manifestations." —*New York Journal of Books*

"Emily Robbins's debut novel is not about Syria so much as dictatorship in general. . . . It is also a lyrical study of love and loss, one not to be overlooked." —*The Globe and Mail*

"[An] extraordinary debut." —*Bustle*

"Deeply affecting . . . Here, Syria is more than a war-torn nation—it's a site of longing, love, and intellectual rigor." —*Hazlitt*

"The shiny gold cover and title caught my eye, but I stayed for the premise. A college student travels to the Middle East to study a famed text of doomed love. Her fascination with language may be what drew her to the country, but it's the political turmoil and the people she meets that really serve to educate her."
—*Book Riot*

"With lyrical precision and sharp psychology, *A Word for Love* asks us to consider the ways one household might become a world, one love might become a universe." —Rebecca Makkai, author of *Music for Wartime*

"Transforms the most impossibly tangled and dehumanizing aspects of the world we live in now into prose so clear and clean you could drink it."
—Kathryn Davis, author of *Duplex* and *The Thin Place*

"*A Word for Love* artfully tells a human story while keeping a mounting conflagration (in Syria and elsewhere) constantly in its frame. Subtle, lapidary, powerful, the novel beautifully evokes the quiet of rooms and the turbulence outside, showing how an innocent evolves into a witness, and how much it costs her, and how much more it costs those she comes to love."
—Zachary Lazar, author of *Sway*

"Bea is a winning choice as a narrator, lending the story vulnerability and authenticity, especially because she is such an empathetic, and often helpless, spectator. With an impressive economy of words, Robbins, formerly a Fulbright Fellow in Syria, tells a story that proves that themes of love, loss, and freedom truly can transcend borders and time." —*Booklist* (starred review)

"Robbins weaves a story complete with exquisite sentences, including descriptions of the Syrian landscape. . . . Bea's fascination with language and the unique characteristics of Arabic add delightful layers to the text. This is a rich, understated novel that offers an absorbing story full of longing, political intrigue, and the beauty found outside the familiar." —*Publishers Weekly*

"This debut serves as a meditation on the many meanings and forms of love, and how words and texts can be used both to love and to harm."
—*Library Journal*

"A lyrical, bittersweet story that raises more questions than it answers, Robbins's debut explores the gaps in translation (both linguistic and cultural), the problems of divided loyalties, and many words for love . . . [A] luminous, bittersweet novel." —*Shelf Awareness*

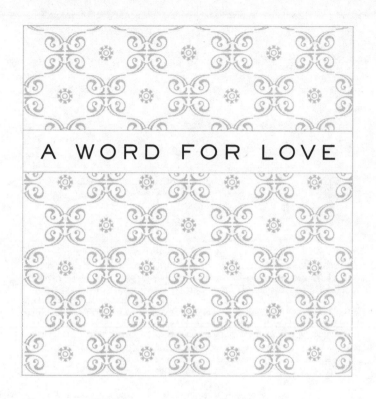

A WORD FOR LOVE

EMILY ROBBINS

RIVERHEAD BOOKS
NEW YORK

RIVERHEAD BOOKS
An imprint of Penguin Random House LLC
375 Hudson Street
New York, New York 10014

First Riverhead hardcover edition: January 2017
First Riverhead trade paperback edition: January 2018
Riverhead hardcover ISBN: 9781594633584
Riverhead trade paperback ISBN: 9780399185854

Printed in the United States of America
1 3 5 7 9 10 8 6 4 2

Book design by Marysarah Quinn

FOR MY PARENTS
AND ARTHUR, WITH LOVE

A WORD FOR LOVE

BEFORE

THE BOX ARRIVED ON MY DOORSTEP, small and unassuming. It was addressed to me, but only with my first name. The letters stood up painfully, without any slant, as if the person who wrote them was not used to writing English. This was my first clue. I thought it might be a box from Madame. I had left some books with her when I lived with her years ago, and ever since, she had been promising to send them. But when I lifted the box up, I found it was too light to contain books. In the corner was a foreign postage stamp, and beside it, an insignia that I recognized as the police's.

I opened it slowly, and papers poured out: poems, printed text messages, calling cards ripped in half. I lifted them and smoothed them; Kleenexes bought by the packet to write on. This was a box from a policeman; he knew the importance of documents. I had once been told that he was a real Qais, which meant a deep lover. I heard a story that he once clipped a poem to the ear of a teddy bear and sent it. The bear was for love. The poem was his document.

I want to record in my hand—Bea, do you remember your Arabic?

I want to record in my hand. Anything I've done after 20-01, 2005, until today, and after today, if it is romantic, it is only for Nisrine. Because I can't speak or do to any girl—only her. There isn't anyone other than her. And I record it here, in my name, too: My name is Adel Ibrahim Ammar Talbani, that's my identification. I'm known to some as Abu Talib, that was my name at the police station. And among the boys, I am Ammar, they call me Ammar. But my name is Adel, and I was a policeman. And I write this to Bea because, like I said, I cannot do for any girl—only Nisrine, and my love for her will never change, if I change it's only for the better. And Bea knows all this, because she knew Nisrine, and Nisrine knew everything, and from my heart, I wish her all happiness.

Adel, 21 January, 20—

I had gone to Adel's country as a student of Arabic, and I returned, six months earlier than expected, thinking that I would never leave home again for a foreign country. Nisrine was my reason. I wanted to lock myself in my room for a long time and not come out, so I couldn't accidentally make trouble for anyone. I tried to bury my guilt. I blamed myself.

*And Bea knows all this, because she knew
Nisrine, and Nisrine knew everything . . .*

The madam of the house where I lived always said that if you can write, it means you have a clear conscience. I took up the policeman's poems, one by one. I sorted through his documents. I laid them all out, so I could see them as I was working. I began this story, in the hope that I could do it justice, and clear my conscience.

MEETING

THE RAINS CAME to the foreign city with red skies. All over, people watched the fiery night above them, brushed their palms across their foreheads and muttered, "Tomorrow will bring rain." The clouds were restless with the wind. The next day rain did not come. Nor the day after.

Two weeks later, though, it came as the people promised. Men at the mosques washed their feet in the rain, catching the water from the faucets with care, one hand holding their coats to shield their heads from the sky. The drops of moisture were stars on their foreheads, shining as they ran down wrinkled faces, into the whites of cloudy eyes. In them the town saw heaven, and it was gray.

For a while, the rains took the power with them. The people in their houses sat in the dark of candlelight. The sky was bright outside. And the planes flying overhead through the night did not know they were passing over a city.

In the morning, the rains were gone and when they cleared,

there was a holiday. The people streamed into the street and watched the leftover water run off the cobblestones. The sun was glowing and pulsing. The water made off with the dust and the stray garbage bags and ran out to the highways and sand hills. Above it were the sigh and flap of rugs as they dried out the windows. Wet coats, strung from hangers on the balconies, leaned low over the morning city.

The rains came, and with them the police. They stood about in the sun after it cleared, tan as wheat, smelling the cobblestones. The police dragged wet sandbags to dry in the sun on the streets. They made a small gray mound, right in the middle of the traffic lane. There was a sweet smell of sandbags drying, and the policemen brought more for the other lanes so, as they were drying, the sandbags made a blockade.

The cars were all stopping by the sandbags and the policemen were leaning against them, checking licenses and back plates. We were seven in the car, coming from the market, and no one had a seat belt. Madame was in the front seat with Abudi, and Baba was driving. Nisrine and I were in the backseat with Lema and Dounia, the little girls. We talked about bribing the policeman.

Madame gathered up our apples and put them in a bag.

"Here, Bea, you give these to the policeman."

I didn't want to.

Madame wasn't listening.

I said, "Here, Nisrine, you give these to the policeman."

We stopped at the sandbags, which stretched from the station to the public garden, and Baba rolled down his window.

"Now, Bea."

Nisrine and I got out of the car, giggling, and handed the bag of apples to the policeman. Then we got back in.

The policeman opened the bag to inspect it. He had blond hair beneath his gray cap; in the sun it was glinting. He looked through Madame's window into the backseat where Nisrine and I sat, giggling.

He checked Baba's license.

"Go through," he said, holding the apples, "go through."

We didn't go far. We rolled past the blockade and parked on the other side, in front of our building. I turned around to look for the policeman.

In the rearview mirror, Baba caught me turning.

Baba said, "I see Bea likes blond men."

In the backseat, Dounia caught my giggling.

Madame said, "Shh, Dounia. It's not nice on young girls to giggle."

Later, I would learn that the blond policeman was also watching. He followed us with his eyes all the way out of our car, and he found us again, five floors up on our balcony, airing our shoes. Dounia's shoes were too small; they were patent-leather white and they almost slipped through the railing. He saw Nisrine bend to retrieve them.

His friends stood around, checking cars and license plates. They wanted to buy cigarettes.

"Come on, Adel," they said to the blond policeman.

But Adel was still holding our apples.

Another car rolled up, and he thought he heard someone giggle in it, so he let that car go through, because he liked the sound.

BEA

MADAME AND I WERE INTRODUCED by an agency that found families for a fee. I was twenty-one and studying abroad from America. Before I came, my university paid the agency and the agency paid Madame my first month's rent, which was US$150. It was Madame's first time as a family-for-a-fee. It was my first time as a paying student in a foreign country.

We lived in an apartment with five rooms and a balcony that looked out over the center of the city. From it, we could see over the gray tops of the buildings, to the large bridge that ran north toward the president's house, to the minarets of the mosques and their green lights at the edges of the highways. Across from us was the police station, which was a tall, gray building like ours, with five stories. From our balcony, we saw the policemen standing guard at each corner of its long, flat roof, legs apart. In the center of the station roof were an open shed and a little turret with a chair and a phone in case the policemen needed to be reached. We could hear them on the phone in the afternoons, ordering up tea. Behind the station, cement buildings lined up in uneven rows, the same way Baba's friends lined up their shoes at the door before they went into the parlor to talk politics. When the men were all inside, Madame and Nisrine and I squatted by the door to straighten their shoes. We brushed dust from the leather tongues. We folded their socks and set them beside the children's, neatly. Madame judged men by their feet; a man who took care of his shoes would take care of his family.

In our apartment, Madame fit herself; her husband, Baba; and Lema, Abudi, and Dounia, who were the children. Lema was fourteen. Abudi was nine. Dounia was four. In the last year, Madame had had two maids who didn't work out, and then Nisrine came from Indonesia, and she also gained me, the American.

For US$150 a month, I got half a bed and fresh food, and the chance to learn a language and literature that I had fallen in love with. If I went out, I got a family who worried until I came home. For half a bed and extra bathwater and extra worry, Madame got rent in American money, which she used to pay Nisrine.

Madame said when you got a maid from Indonesia, she came with a black bag and a white veil. That was what Nisrine was wearing when Madame got her, and everyone expected it. They drove up to a crumbling part of town. It was Madame and Baba and the children. The agency man had Nisrine's passport. He handed it to Baba and said to hide it where she couldn't get to it, and she knew no calls home, and if there were any problems, call him. His number was in the passport.

In this country, the money exchange only went one way. You could change US dollars into local money, but you couldn't change local money into dollars. It was illegal to change local money, and in this city, only the local money could be spent, but you couldn't travel with it outside the country, that was also illegal, so dollars were the way most international business got done, and people, who were paid only in local money, were always short on dollars, and always scrambling to get some, even when their international business was only an Indonesian maid, like Nisrine.

Nisrine got US$125 a month, plus a fee to the agency, and so Madame was always in need of dollars, and she was always running out. That was why Madame got me, to take care of her problems with the currency.

Nisrine also had to pay her agency. To come here, she'd borrowed her wages for one year, up front, and she was saving up to build a house when she returned home, so she, too, always needed money. She got small gifts from guests of the family.

"Here's for your girl," said Madame's aunt, and handed her a bill in a thin scarf.

"Buy yourself something special," said Baba's cousin, and handed her two silver coins.

The guests didn't bring gifts for Madame, but there was always something for Nisrine, and it made Madame happy. "See how good they are to her?" she said. "They think of her even before they think of me!"

Because I was foreign, Madame was always worrying about me, like she did about Nisrine, though in different ways. With Nisrine, Madame worried about communication. She worried Nisrine would invite strange men to the house, or whether she'd mistaken the iodine for bleach, or if she'd used enough detergent on the pans. "Watch her, Bea," Madame said to me, and I sat in the kitchen, watching to make sure Nisrine took the white part off the oranges we ate.

"How many brothers and sisters do you have, Nisrine?"

"Nineteen."

"Nineteen?"

Nisrine had hands like birds. They picked at the white part. In Nisrine's country, there was a story about a heroine who turned into a bird. She loved the rainbow, so she flew away to the sky, and never returned home. At Madame's, we were often telling stories.

"How many brothers and sisters do you have?" Nisrine asked me.

"None."

"None?" And I knew from the way she said it that here, "none" was as strange as "nineteen."

Nisrine finished two oranges, and Lema came to take them to the living room. When she was done, Nisrine got out her photos to show me. They were all of her with her husband and child, and she wasn't wearing a veil. She had left when her child was one. Now, he was almost two. We tried to guess which words he would be speaking.

"Book," I said.

Nisrine looked at me. "Bea, you like books?"

"Animal," I guessed.

"I like animals."

"Love," I guessed.

Nisrine guessed, "World."

. . .

I had a picture, too, to show Nisrine. It was of my parents before they were married, and my mother looked like me. This was to remind me that it was still possible to get a boyfriend, even with birds'-nest hair.

Nisrine took the picture from me. "Your mother looks very nice," she said. Then she asked, "You want to know what my mother looks like?" and puffed out her cheeks.

"You mean, fat?" I was unsure.

She laughed. "In my family, we're all fat. We like too much to eat."

I looked at Nisrine. She had a slender waist and legs that rose perfectly beneath her pajamas, like young trees. When she laughed, it shook her breasts, not her belly.

Later, I would come to see this joke as Nisrine's own special kind of joke, her special luxury. Madame's apartment was small, and we were many; each of us learned to take our luxuries. Madame's husband, Baba, slept at any time, anywhere, through anything. This was his luxury. Guests came over at four in the afternoon, and Madame served tea around him, watched television around him, balanced the tray on his stomach, and he didn't wake from his place on the sofa, snoring.

Mine was my books, and my love of romance. I learned to bury myself in an Arabic book at Madame's, and to daydream so deeply, it didn't matter what was around me; in this way, I took time for myself.

Nisrine told jokes. She made faces at the children, "I'm a monster!" which made them laugh, because they knew she wasn't.

I told her, "You're not fat."

"Because I'm not old and rich. Someday, I'll be rich and have a restaurant and a big house, and then my child and I will sit and do nothing but eat."

MADAME WORRIED ABOUT ME, like she did about Nisrine. She worried I'd touch diseased animals because my mother was a veterinarian, and about my femininity and my unpierced ears, and because after we gave him apples, I began to notice the blond policeman. He was always guarding on the roof of the station, a slender gold line, like an Arabic *alif,* against the blue sky

If he still had our apples, he could throw one, and I could reach over our balcony rail and catch it, we were close enough.

In the kitchen, Madame grabbed my ear to distract me. "Why don't you pierce your ears, Bea? See Nisrine? Nisrine has pierced ears."

Dounia ran in to steal a potato chip. Madame stopped her. She ran back out.

"See Dounia? Dounia has pierced ears. Dounia's my baby, she was a C-section. When I had her, it burned so much I couldn't see. I kept saying, Where's my baby? I felt like I didn't have a baby."

When I first arrived, Madame sent Nisrine into the bathroom to count out two squares of toilet paper, which was how much I should use when I peed. Madame and Nisrine didn't need any. There was an orange hose beside the toilet that they used to wash when they needed it.

Nisrine helped me lug my bag into the bedroom. There were two pillows on the bed, one for Madame's daughter Lema, and one for me. Nisrine slept on a mat on the floor.

Madame had emptied out two dresser drawers for me. In one, Nisrine helped me put my books. In the other, I tried to stuff all my clothes, but it wouldn't shut all the way, so she intervened.

"This drawer is for underwear, Bea. Books go in the parlor."

I said, "It's OK, no problem."

Lema was Madame's oldest, she had shared a bed her whole life. I grew up alone with my mother in a restored Victorian house. Before Madame's, I had never shared a bed, or dresser drawers, or watched to see if the maid took the white part off the oranges correctly. There hadn't been a maid.

I said again to Madame, "It's OK. Here, I know where to find them."

We all stood waiting. Finally, Nisrine said, "Don't worry, Bea, we'll fix it."

So, she smoothed flat my underwear and put it between the pages. Madame took all my shirts and hung them in the closet, so my books could stay in the drawer, near me.

I was in this new country to study. I'd come, hoping to find a certain text at the National Library, and I'd also applied to the local university, but they still hadn't gotten back to me, so in the meantime, I sat in the kitchen and tried to practice my Arabic typing.

The blond policeman out the window distracted me.

He was always laughing and joking with his friends. Bring her flowers, I imagined he told them, Don't cheat!

While I daydreamed, the children played with my computer. They pushed the A button over and over again. They pushed Delete.

Madame said, "If you can write, it means you have a clear conscience."

We watched the children push the E button.

Out the window, blond hair gleamed like fresh turmeric.

Dounia was too good with Delete, she'd deleted all my work, so Madame got out a belt from Baba's closet.

"Hold her down, Nisrine."

Abudi and Lema and I sat in the kitchen, listening. Afterwards, Dounia shut herself in the bedroom and wouldn't come out.

I lurked before the door, wondering.

Nisrine said, "It's OK, Bea. You need something? You can go in."

When we knocked to get my bag, Dounia was singing.

BUT DESPITE THE TROUBLE with Delete, Madame's apartment was exciting to live in. On Thursdays, Baba's friends came over and sat for long hours in the parlor with the windows open, talking about the government. The parlor had low, ornate chairs lined up along the walls and small carved tables to put the juice on. Because all the chairs were along the wall, the men sat far away from one another. Between them was the wide room and soft carpet, and they had to speak loudly across the carpet to be heard.

When the men were there, the rest of us weren't allowed to go in. Every now and then Baba opened the door and walked all the way into the kitchen to ask Madame for something. She sent Nisrine to serve the food, and when Nisrine came back, we wanted to know all about the men: How many? What did they look like? Because he was the only boy, Abudi went in and sat with his father. Baba's hand was very large on Abudi's shoulder. It guided him to a seat on an uncle's knee. It kept him from fidgeting. Abudi had delicate shoulders, like a girl.

One Thursday, Baba's best friend, Amo Nasir, came over with his wife, Moni, and then we were all allowed to sit with them in the living room listening, while Baba and Amo Nasir gave a phone interview for TV.

Amo Nasir had a long tongue and teeth like goose eggs, and he was known all over as this country's Nelson Mandela, because he'd spent so many years in jail. His shoes stayed on the floor beside him instead of at the door like the rest of our shoes, and he held the phone in one hand and the TV remote in the other, and gave his interview live while we listened, one bare foot keeping time across the conversation.

"We can't even sleep with our wives without the government knowing," Amo Nasir said into the phone and on TV.

His wife, Moni, elbowed Madame, "Oof, who says I let him sleep with me?"

This was my first hint about Baba's politics. I sat stoically with the women in the living room, eating potato chips that Nisrine brought us, until Madame winked, and then Moni and Nisrine and I all got up at once and floated down the hall like light into the bedroom, where Madame showed us her lingerie.

She brought out the pieces one by one. She smoothed them across her arm. The tags were all in English. They said, SEXY! in pink letters. They said, KEEP IT HOT!

"Come here, Bea," Madame said. "Is this one pretty?"

It was sheer and white.

"Look here, Bea. My baba and mama got me this one."

It was sheer and black.

I fingered Madame's lingerie, feeling the silk slip through my fingers, measuring the lace against my skin. Would I wear lace like this someday? When Madame was done with a piece, she handed it to Nisrine to hold, high against her chest, so it didn't touch the floor. Nisrine was shorter than Madame and me; what came to our thighs came to her knees. She posed before the window, making the lingerie beautiful.

Madame moved to the dresser that she shared with me, opened up her drawer, and pulled out a box of edible underwear.

"What does it say, Bea?"

The box was all in English. It was flavored chocolate with strawberries. It said, EDIBLE UNDERWEAR. ALL STRINGS, PARTS, ATTACHMENTS EDIBLE.

"Mama, where did you buy this?"

But Madame wanted to know if there was an expiration date. There wasn't one. She wanted to know what else it said.

It said, THE MORE IT'S LICKED, THE BETTER IT TASTES!

Madame sighed. "All that lingerie I bought, I haven't used any of it since the unrest."

Abudi came in. Madame took the box from me.

Abudi asked, "What's that?"

"Nothing," Madame told him. "Where's Baba? I thought you were with Baba. Or Nisrine, you should be watching Abudi." She carefully placed the box in the drawer, among her sweaters. I wondered if edible underwear melted in the heat.

When it was time to go home, Moni wouldn't get in the car with her husband until he'd started it, to make sure there was no bomb inside. She was joking with him; she thought after his interview the government would want to get rid of him. Nisrine and I watched from the balcony while she waited, her toes over the curb.

Nisrine poked me. "It's OK, Bea, you can laugh. She's only joking."

"Haha." But I felt a hairline crack of doubt. I wasn't used to jokes about car bombs.

Across from us, lamps bloomed along the walls of the police station, where even at night the policemen stood guarding.

Nisrine looked where I was looking. "Do you like them, Bea?"

I did, but I was suddenly shy.

She said, "It's OK to like here."

"Do you?"

But before she could answer, Dounia came out. Nisrine lifted her up, and we three leaned over the railing, into a dark city.

Nisrine told us a story. It was about a heroine who dropped a spindle from heaven, and so had to make her way down to earth to retrieve it. The skyline was the map of her journey. When she got to earth, she found the spindle had landed in the lap of a man, and so she stayed with him. For this reason the horizon is a line, not a circle.

"Why didn't she go home?" Dounia asked about the heroine.

"I don't know. I'm sure she wanted to."

"How did she keep from getting lonely?"

Nisrine thought for a moment. "I don't know, ask Bea."

I had not felt very lonely here so far, but I didn't know how you kept from it. I wanted to know. I thought of the heroine and the man. "Maybe she liked someone."

Nisrine gave me a funny look. For a moment, I wondered if she liked someone. Or, wanted to like someone? We had just talked about liking.

She had her husband at home in Indonesia.

Nisrine said, "I suppose the heroine had to grow a very big heart. Big enough to fit her home, and the new place where she lived."

Dounia asked, "How do you do that?"

"I don't know, I'm still practicing. Do you know, Bea?"

I didn't know, either.

I leaned on the balcony, feeling for my heart, and her heart.

We three leaned out, toward the lights of mosques like small beacons.

Nisrine made a face at Dounia. "I'm hungry, I'm going to eat you," which made Dounia laugh. Then she pointed down. "Look."

Below us on the street, Amo Nasir was laughing. His noise floated up to us. He opened his car door for Baba, who got in, and the two men drove once around the block, teeth huge and white in the dark like jasmine, laughing, to prove to their wives they were safe, there was no bomb.

AFTER AMO NASIR LEFT, Madame turned on the gas, and we all rushed to heat water and take our baths before it turned off for the night.

I helped Madame line up white scarves, smallest to largest, on the radiator to tie on our heads when our baths were done. The scarves were so our hair would dry flat and straight. When you were wearing the bath scarf it meant your hair was not dry, and you couldn't go sit out on the balcony.

This was the sort of rule that it sometimes seemed strange to have to follow. But I did, and when I looked around I saw that Nisrine and Lema both followed it, too, and that at Madame's, rules like this were taken for granted. So, I tried to take them for granted, too.

I asked Madame, "Do they always make car bomb jokes?"

"Of course, Bea. Didn't you laugh? Haha."

I followed Nisrine into the bedroom, and we both hurried to take off our day clothes and put on our pajamas, before the children finished brushing their teeth.

Nisrine slipped off first her outer veil, then her inner, and laid them on her mat in the corner. She took a brush from the children's dresser to run in long sweeps through her hair. "Shh, don't tell," she told me about the brush.

Her hair was thick and straight; from the static of the veil, it stood up in some parts. She wetted her palm with her tongue to smooth the runaway strands. "I have to brush it every night," she explained. "The veil makes me sweat, and it gets oily."

I rarely saw Nisrine without her veil, because it was part of her uniform. She wore it even at night to sleep, and when she didn't, she slept with the covers over her head, for warmth. Sometimes, when Dounia had a nightmare, she burrowed into the covers with Nisrine on the mat on the floor, and that was how I would find them in the morning.

Now, I watched her hair swaying, and thought it was beautiful. The ends that stuck out reminded me of tributaries on a blue-black river. I wetted my palm, too, to help her smooth them. They moved when she did, restless.

I never brushed my own hair; if I did, it would frizz.

. . .

Because Nisrine wanted her own house, she loved this one. She liked to say what she would change if it were hers, and what she would keep: the light, coming in through the window. The gold-framed calligraphy: *Allah*. She would change the locks, so you could get out from the inside (except the bathroom, Madame's doors only locked from the outside), and she would make a back door.

"Where I'm from," Nisrine told me, "back doors are important." They were the entrance friends used. The front door was stiff and formal; in some homes, it didn't even open, it was just for show. "If I had a house like this, people wouldn't know what to do." In Nisrine's town, you entered through the back door to show your closeness.

A door to show closeness; I liked the sound of this.

I was already beginning to see how important it was at Madame's, to feel close. So far, we had rarely gone out; we stayed in the apartment and had one another.

My house in the United States was old and echoey. I sometimes ran up and down the stairs, through a long hallway, to find my mother. I thought about my friends from home, or from university: What had we used to show our closeness? Phone calls?

I looked at Nisrine, and wondered what two women in Madame's apartment might do, to show they were close.

Nisrine said, "Come on, Bea, we have to hurry."

"We do?"

"The children will come back."

So, I stopped thinking of doors and home and instead turned my back, and Nisrine turned her back, in the small room, so we could undress in private together: wrinkled shirts, grabbed pants, the last call to prayer out our window, the sense of urgency to finish before the children, who never knocked, came running in.

LIKE I SAID, I was in this new country to study. So, in the afternoon Madame unlocked the door for me, and let me go out to the National Library, just to see.

The library was a large cement structure with a statue of the president out front. It was surrounded on all sides by a cement garden, and security. Walking there, I passed down small alleys that Madame said used to be lemon groves. Now, they held used car-parts stores and juice stands, where flies and the car-parts men both stopped to drink.

I walked in boldly and presented my student ID.

The librarian at the desk didn't seem to notice me.

I presented it again.

"Yes?"

I said, "I've come to study."

There were no computers in the library, only a card catalogue. Students and scholars weren't allowed around the books. The woman gave me a note card to fill out, with my name, my purpose, and the titles I would need. I put down the title of the text I'd come to this country for. When I was done, the librarian took my purse from me, and led me empty-handed to a small open room in the center of the stacks with wooden slats like a cage all around. This was where I would wait for my book.

Inside the cage were five scholars with long beards. None of them had books. None of them acknowledged me.

I sat down at an empty wooden desk to wait. I could see my purse hanging on a hook beside the librarian's head.

The scholars passed the time by reciting poetry, and verses of the Quran. They held their hands palm up, toward God, the way Madame's children held their palms when they were asking for something.

After an hour of waiting, I went to the front of the wooden cage and waved at the librarian.

She didn't seem to notice.

"Excuse me?" My voice echoed across the empty stacks.

"Yes?"

I said, "I'm waiting for a book. Has it arrived?"

The librarian told me that when it arrived, she would call me.

So, I sat down to wait again.

I waited and waited.

When it was time for the library to close, the librarian opened the door of the cage and let the scholars and me out. None of us had our books. I went up to the librarian to ask about mine again.

She said, "Come back tomorrow, we'll get it for you."

"I waited all day. I was hoping for it today."

The librarian looked annoyed. "Good things take patience. Didn't they teach you that when they taught you to read?"

BUT DESPITE THE LACK OF BOOKS, or the strange jokes, or, like Nisrine said, feeling lonely, what I remember most about those days is their beauty.

In the mornings, sunlight streamed through the kitchen windows, refracting sharply off glasses of milk as if it could break them. Nisrine boiled the milk and skimmed off the skin. In each cup, she stirred one teaspoon of Milo, and the children wanted more, but they had no time because there was a rush to dress for school. We took Dounia's hair in our hands to braid it, and Nisrine was the fastest. She gathered the short hairs underneath and wet a brush to remove the tangles before braiding, in a hurry, exhilarated, while I kneeled beneath Dounia and tied her shoes.

Baths at Madame's were an adventure. They happened once a week. Baba was the head of the house, so he bathed first, even though he was the most dirty, and made the tub dirty. Madame sent Nisrine in afterwards with soap and a rag to clean it, quickly, so the rest of us could bathe, youngest to oldest because the youngest went to bed first. Afterwards, we lounged in our bath scarves, talking. Madame was the only one allowed to take the scarves off. She slipped a cold finger under the side to feel my hair.

"Not yet," and even though I was twenty-one, paying rent, I was consigned to keep playing with the children in the living room, with the radiator on even on warm days, so we would not catch a cold.

. . .

Nisrine had too much hair. Hers was the most beautiful and the straightest, but also the thickest.

She was the maid, so she bathed last, and last time, she'd used too much water on her hair, it took too long, so Madame told me to cut it.

She brought me the scissors and held Nisrine's hair in two handfuls, which made it uneven.

I didn't want to. I said to Madame, "I don't think I'm good at this."

Madame wasn't listening. She watched the open bathroom door to make sure Dounia didn't make a mess of the tub.

We were used to doing what Madame asked, without complaining; to taking our turns standing before her, while she tied white scarves like snowflakes on our just-washed heads.

I looked down at Nisrine to see if all of us were joking.

"OK, here we go!" I joked. "It's a salon, who's up next? Chop chop."

Nisrine sat very still beneath me. She reached up to brush away a loose strand, then brought her hand back down.

I said again to Madame, "You do it, Mama. I don't think I'm good at this."

Madame just handed me Nisrine's hair in two ponytails. Its weight surprised me.

"Nisrine, do you mind?"

Nisrine had been my first guide here. We had been in the process, she and I, of becoming close.

She sat very still. After a moment, she cleared her throat. "No."

Madame said, "Come on, Bea, someone has to do it."

So, I took each handful of hair and cut it at the nape of the neck, just where Madame showed me.

When it was done, Nisrine went to the bathroom to look, and came out wearing her veil. She and Madame and I gathered up her hair and threw it off the balcony. It floated down like smoke in the night to our garden, where it caught in the bushes.

Madame said, "It's OK, Bea. I'll take her to the stylist when I take the girls."

The next morning I made the bed and did the dishes, which made everyone uncomfortable. Nisrine took my bed apart and made it up again.

"Let me do it, Bea. You don't know how to do it."

I said, "It's OK, no problem."

Madame came in. "It's OK, Bea. Nisrine will do it. Don't you have to study?"

"It's OK, no problem."

When Nisrine was young, her hair had been short; she'd told me her parents cut it often, because they believed that way, when it grew, it would grow back thicker. That had been when she was young.

Nisrine said, "Yes. Don't you have to study, Bea? You don't know how to do it. Leave it for me."

AT MADAME'S there were certain things we talked about, and certain things we knew to leave.

Madame was always asking about my mother. She wanted to know all about how my mother became a veterinarian, and my lack of siblings, and my favorite foods to eat. My mother called up from America once every other week, and when she did, Madame invited her and invited me, even though I was already here.

"Say hello to your mother, Bea. Don't be an ingrate. Pass the greetings on! And give her a kiss. Come bring your mother to visit. Tell her our house is always open, she's a guest. You're not a guest, you're family. Really, you're family. I see you not as American; you dress long, you speak like we speak, Bea, when are you going to get married? I want to see the children you turn out, Bea, when your studies are done, you don't have to leave. Tell your mother to come here instead. Welcome! It's boring here without you, *mashallah*. You get used to someone, they live with you, you love them, and then they're gone."

When I called up America, Madame gave all her love to my mother and my unborn children, and if she was feeling generous, she said, "Fine, even your father, give him my love, it's OK with me if it's OK with you."

When my mother called me up, I gave my mother's love to Madame and the children, and if I was feeling generous, I gave her love to Nisrine. To Baba I gave nothing. On the phone, we didn't mention husbands by name. Madame didn't mention the health of my father, and she didn't ask about my studies. If she did ask, I would have told her: My father lived in New York. I saw him every summer.

I liked Arabic for its precision, the way the words leafed out like spring from three-letter roots. In Arabic, there is a root for knowledge, and from this root, you can make the words for world and tenderness. There is a root for friendship; from it, you can make the word for being true.

In the dresser drawer that Madame emptied out for me, between my book pages and my underwear, I had lists and lists of the texts I wanted to study, and I had other lists of famous places in the city I wanted to go: the biblical street called Straight; the famous Knights' Castle; the National Library, in it were texts you couldn't find anywhere else.

When I decided to come here, the study abroad officer wanted me to know it might be hard. This wasn't an official program, it would just be me. I'd have to find my own Arabic teacher, and work on an independent research project. If it was good, then I could get credit when I returned home.

But, I wasn't thinking about hard. I was thinking about the Arabic root for togetherness, how from this root, you could make the words for university, and Friday prayer.

Before I left, my mother worried for me. "Don't you want to go on an official program?" she asked.

On an official program, I would be with a group of students, and we'd have scheduled classes.

But this country was less well-known, and its government did not get along with the US government, so it didn't offer official programs. I wanted to be in this country.

I dreamed of fitting in, in an Arabic-speaking family. And, there was another reason.

My Arabic professors in America all talked about one ancient text that made everyone who read it cry, it was that astonishing. This is the test of a language: you know it when it moves you. Someday, when I had studied enough, I wanted to go to the National Library and read that text, and then I would cry, because Arabic moved me. That was why I had come to this place.

AT MADAME'S, we were always talking about beauty. In the evening, Lema turned on the TV and wanted to know which singer was pretty. "Do you like him, Bea?" He was fat and ugly. "Do you like him, Bea?"

None of us liked the TV singers, they were all a little fat and ugly, so Lema turned the game outside on the police. We sat by the window, watching them at the station.

"Do you like him, Bea?" But I didn't like him, he wasn't tall like the blond one. "Do you like him, Bea?" After a moment, Lema turned away in frustration. "Bea only likes the blond one because her hair is light like his."

Lema's hair was brown and as curly as mine, but you wouldn't know it, because she was always straightening it before she left the house, even though when she went out, she always wore a veil. Lema had dark hair and dark eyes, and her skin was darker than Madame's and mine, though not as dark as Abudi's. There is a word in Arabic for Abudi's skin, it is called *sumr,* and it means tan, the color of sand hills, or thyme leaves when they're drying, or almost as dark as Nisrine.

When Baba came home, he wanted to know all about what we were doing, and it made him laugh. "Careful, Bea, the blond one is famous. Everyone knows all about him."

I wanted to know what everyone knew.

"His name is Adel. They say he's a real Qais. His father paid good money to make him city police."

"See?" Lema said. "Bea goes for blond and she gets corruption." When it was Lema's turn to pick the prettiest policeman, she only liked the brown-haired ones.

In my drawer were long shirts and loose pants out of respect, but at Madame's everyone else dressed tight, even Nisrine. Madame shot an appraising look at me. She cinched my shirt from behind and rolled up my sleeves. She pushed back my hair, let it hang down, squeezed my unpierced ears, lightly. "Have you *ever* had a boyfriend, Bea?"

The most beautiful one in our apartment was Nisrine. She had large dark eyes, and you could see the bulge of her thick hair beneath her veil before I cut it.

Her face was perfectly round and smooth, and every now and then a wisp of hair would come out of her veil and curl across her forehead like a crooked finger. She was beautiful, and she chopped very fine parsley.

The night after I cut her hair, while we played prettiest policeman, Nisrine did the laundry. She went to Madame in the kitchen.

"I found dirt in her underwear."

Madame said, "She'll learn, she'll learn."

Nisrine said, "She's old enough to know better."

Madame said, "She'll learn, she'll learn. Bea, when you go to the bathroom, you use water, then paper, not just paper, that's dirty, you understand?"

"I know, I'm sorry, Nisrine."

"See, Nisrine? She knows, she's sorry. She'll learn."

MADAME SAID, "Don't change in front of the window."

She nodded at the police station.

"They can see in. And don't open the door to strangers. You don't know who is out there. The president's brother opened his door, that's how he became a martyr." The front door didn't have a handle, only a key. Madame locked the door from the outside whenever she left the apartment. That way, we couldn't open it to strangers while she was gone.

"And only change when you are alone. Tell us when you want to change, and we'll leave. You want to change now?" She pushed

Abudi out of the bedroom in front of her so Nisrine and I could change alone with the blinds closed, because we were both foreign.

When Madame left, Nisrine opened a window.

Madame's apartment was in the center of the city, but I knew Nisrine had never really seen the city, because like me and like Madame, she rarely left the apartment. What we knew of this place was the air above us when we went out on the balcony. We knew the fresh cheese that Baba brought from the market.

On the dresser beside the mirror was a can of deodorant. Nisrine sprayed the deodorant and twirled around in it like perfume.

Between us were the open window and my embarrassment about her hair. Nisrine was twirling and twirling.

After a while, she said, "Here, Bea, you want some deodorant?"

"Yes, please."

So she sprayed some for me, and we both twirled around in it.

Dounia opened the door on us. The room smelled of damp tile floors and deodorant. Dounia started to shut the door, but Nisrine sprayed some for her, so she came in, too, and the three of us twirled around.

We lived by a police station, so we were always watched by idle men. I once climbed with Abudi to our own flat roof, to check our water tank when we thought the neighbors were stealing. From up there, Abudi and I could see everything and we, like the police, were the center of all of it, we with our indoor slippers and pajama pants, they with their tilted caps and young boredom. We were the heart of the city, alive and beating. We looked out over the world and watched the small breaths of plastic bags on the sidewalk, the in-out of the bags' bellies. We looked over the roof-tops to white satellite dishes peppered with dirt, tangled up in antennas and telephone wires, and the absence of birds.

Baba had said, *His name is Adel. They say he's a real Qais. His father paid good money to make him city police.*

I didn't yet know about Adel, but I knew about Qais. He was a young man from a famous Bedouin tribe. His love story went back for generations, and everyone here knew it and looked to it, the way in English we look to Romeo and Juliet. In the story, Qais falls in love with the beautiful Leila, and writes her poems. He sings songs outside her tent. He falls so deeply in love, and he is so open with his love, that the tribe stops calling him Qais, and instead calls him Crazy for Leila.

This is the story I had come here to read that made everyone who read it cry. The astonishing text.

In Qais's time, love poetry was dangerous, it was a threat to morality. When Leila's father found out about Qais's poems, he married his daughter off to another man far away, and Qais was banished to the wilderness. For the rest of his life, Qais wandered the desert; he still wrote poems for Leila, and he missed her so much that he forgot his own name, and would only answer to Crazy for Leila. He lived by his lover's name.

I always liked Qais's story for the romance of it, and the way names worked. Qais lost his lover's body, but he gained her name. I had never had a romance like Qais's, but as a foreigner, I understood the feeling of being outside yourself, of looking in the mirror and wanting to belong to someone else. I wanted that, sometimes, too.

. . .

In the bedroom, we were twirling. Nisrine put a hand on Dounia's hip. Then, after a moment, she put a hand on my hip. Her hand was cool like onions, or green tile. It's OK for now, her hand seemed to say. We haven't really made up.

"I'm sorry, Nisrine."

"I know."

His name is Adel.

I had an Arabic teacher in America named Adel. My teacher's name came from the root *ayn-dal-lam,* which meant balanced, or fair. For Americans, it is a hard name to pronounce because of the letter *ayn:* you have to feel your throat click when you say it. But my Arabic teacher in America always said I got his name just right.

At Madame's, we did what we were told. Nisrine had not wanted me to cut her hair, but she had allowed it, because she didn't feel she had a choice.

I had not wanted to do it, but I did.

The room grew wide, and then close, and Dounia blended with Nisrine, and I blended with Dounia—

"Nisrine, you're so pretty!"

"I'm pretty? Your eyes are the pretty." Which was a saying, about the subjective nature of beauty. Like the name *Adel*, which meant balanced, this saying added fairness to beauty. It meant, I'm pretty because you see me as pretty, I wouldn't be pretty without your eyes—

Adel. I'd always liked that name.

BORDER GUARD

BABA WAS RIGHT, everyone did know about Adel. Now, it's hard to remember a time I didn't know about him, too. But over the next weeks, when I asked Baba, or the children, or women in the garden, they all told the same story. What they didn't tell, this box of Adel's documents before me has since helped me to imagine.

BEFORE HE WAS A POLICEMAN, Adel was in the military. This country required two years of service from its men, but Adel didn't feel forced, he wanted to go. He wanted to fly in the air force; he was strong and good-looking and had romantic ideas of service.

Instead, he was made a border guard. There were wars in the neighboring country, and refugees were moving in. They made long lines before the guards at the border. They brought their foods and their bread, and all the unfinished apartments in this city were finished very quickly, because the refugees needed homes to live in. The locals complained about rising prices. Locals here never had money. The young men, Adel's friends, complained mostly, because they wanted to buy apartments and marry, but all the apartments were going to the refugees.

Adel was a native of this country because his father was, even though his mother, while still Arab, was foreign. She was from the neighboring country, and after thirty years she still spoke with the neighboring country's accent, which she gave, despite himself, to her son. Growing up, Adel tried hard to be rid of the accent. Through school and with women, it brought him teasing. He felt not at all foreign, he felt deeply of this place, and in his head he could hear so clearly what it sounded like to be of this place. Yet, he still retained traces of his mother's throaty vowels and round *g* sounds, especially when he was emotional or had been drinking.

I suppose for someone from the United States, this might be like growing up in the North, but inheriting from your parent an accent of the South.

ON THE BORDER, Adel stood around with the other guards and checked the refugees coming in. A man got out of the car and put a steadying hand on his belongings. He motioned his wife and children to face the window so Adel could count them.

"Children, how many?" Adel asked. It sounded foreign. He should have said, How many children?

"Five," said the man, and it sounded foreign, too, just like him.

Adel looked around to see if the other guards had noticed.

"Five?"

Like his father, Adel was of this place.

"Five." But his voice sounded just like them.

Adel felt the sun behind him.

"*Allah khalik,*" said the man, which was a foreign saying.

"Pass through," Adel said. And because the words "pass" and "through" had no telltale *g* or full vowel sounds, he repeated them again. "Pass through, pass through," he said, instead of *God be with you.*

There was a tin barracks from World War I to one side of the border control, and it was always rusting and baking, and no one leaned on the walls because they got hot in the sun and burned. The guards slept in the tin barracks. Inside, it was long and narrow and windowless. From his bed at one end, Adel looked out over fifty beds to the other end. It was not wide enough for two beds in a row, so they slept lined up, head to toe, one by one by one, with an aisle to the right for passing. In the night, the air came through to chill them.

The other guards were Adel's friends. In the evenings between their shifts they terrorized the duty-free, which had all the foreign brands. When they came in, the clerk always got out Trident gum and shared it around with them. There were commerce laws; the border guards weren't allowed to buy anything.

Adel and his friends wandered around the empty store to the cigarette aisle. Adel's mother liked Gauloises. He opened the shiny cardboard box and took out a pack for her. He felt his money in his border guard's pocket. They wandered through the perfume aisle, and took the long way to the checkout line.

The clerk didn't want to sell him anything.

"It's not legal."

His friends said about Adel, "He is the law."

"He'll step over the border and come back, haha."

"I can't just sell to anyone."

Adel, border guard, chewed his free Trident gum. At home, his mother liked new appliances from Europe.

He placed two bills on the counter.

"I don't accept local money. Dollars or euros."

"They're for my mother."

"Look," said the clerk, "you want more gum? Here's another pack. Take one home to your children. Look, here's another for your mom."

"I'm an honest man," Adel said, and walked out. His friends followed him. It was the first time he had done something like this. On the counter were his money and the gum. His mother's cigarettes were in his hand.

At night, the guards lay head to toe in their barracks, talking.

"Adel loves the foreigners," said Adel's friend.

"Do you love the foreigners, Adel?"

"No, I don't gov the foreigners."

"Yes he does. Say love."

"Gov."

"I'm going to hit you every time you speak like a foreigner. Maybe then you'll learn."

Adel said, "I don't love them."

"Very good. You see? He doesn't love them."

But he spoke like them.

"Do you know who my father is?"

Adel's father was of this place. Adel was, too. But, he spoke like *them*.

Adel lasted two months. He had dimples of confidence, and a voice that made others listen. He was not so tall, but he walked tall, and with precision.

In his youth, he had liked to look out over the desert, and imagine what lay beyond it. Then, the border happened.

His voice became gruff and quick. His smile embarrassed him. Even the refugees distrusted him.

So, he called his parents.

"What, Adel," his mother asked, "they don't like you?"

"They love me. They think I'm a refugee."

"What's the matter, Adel?"

(And here, I begin to see where poetry, *the real Qais,* comes in.)

His mother was far away, the whole desert lay between them. He looked for a connection.

"Mama, are you looking through the window? Look at the sky. You have the sky in your view?"

"Adel, if you're unhappy, you can tell me."

Through the phone, Adel made kissing sounds.

"Did they make it?" he asked. "I'll try again. *Kiss kiss*. Did they arrive?"

His mother said, "You want me to talk to your father?"

"I'll try again. Did you hear them? *Kiss kiss*. For your right cheek. *Kiss kiss*, for your left. Here's for your forehead, Mama, did you hear it?" A whole country divided them, but the same sky was above them.

His mother said, "I'll talk to your father."

Adel said, "If you heard it, then it arrived."

After two months Adel's father, who had connections with the government, paid 28,000 lire and Adel was transferred to the Central Police Station to serve out his time. Here, there were no tin barracks that shone and baked in summer. There were no runs, except for cigarettes and errands. A policeman during the day, Adel came home the first night to his parents' house, and doubly loved his mother's cooking.

"*Taqburni hayati*," his mother said, which was a local saying. A mother said it when she especially loved her son. "*Taqburni hayati*," she said again, and kissed him on both cheeks. It meant, I love you so much, you are my lifeline. I love you so much, I hope you will be the one to bury me, when I am gone.

AT THE STATION, Adel paced the roof the way he must have paced the halls of his own home, as if everyone liked him. He looked down over dusty streets and a little garden. Just as police were guardians over the peace of this city, so he was guardian of these streets and this garden.

Beside the garden was our balcony and behind it were our windows. If Adel looked down from his post, he would see Dounia playing in the kitchen. He might watch to see she didn't fall onto the hot stove, or hit her head. He would see me with my book at the table and behind me, Nisrine, chopping our parsley. The green of the parsley came away on her fingers, like spring.

From the way he smiled at us through the window, I thought his job must please him. Everything below was his to guard, and that guarding had a special meaning. As if all this were his because he looked down on it from the rooftop. As if we, too, were his to watch over, to protect and keep.

LEARNING

AT MADAME'S we were always cleaning, because there was always dust. The dust blew in from the deserts and the salt mines to cover the streets. In the winter it got cold, but the cold didn't seem to settle the dust. In the spring there were hot, dark winds that beat the trees along the broad main streets and blew the dust up. The hot winds could make you sick and superstitious. They blew in enough sand to settle on the city and last until next spring. The sand coated your shoes. If you went without socks, it got between your toes and coated your ankles. It was the reason there were indoor shoes and outdoor shoes, and indoor sweats and outdoor jeans, and the outdoor shoes and the outdoor jeans stayed at the door so they didn't track in dust.

Madame handed me a porous rock. "Go wash your feet." And I sat with the children on the balcony running the hose, the porous rock in one hand and the soap in the other to wash our feet, but the dust wouldn't come off. We washed and washed. Nisrine came out and took the rock from us and rubbed our feet, but even she couldn't get it off.

So Madame discarded my flip-flops. They were low class, anyway. They encouraged dust. It would be better if I didn't take the bus, because the bus was full of dust. It would be better if I didn't leave the house, except when necessary, because outside was so full of dust.

IN FEBRUARY, there were rallies. This country had occupied its neighbor for some time. Now, citizens of our neighboring country were protesting; they wanted independence, their own democracy.

In response, the government held its own rallies, in support of the president. We knew they would happen because we received text messages on our mobile phones:

CONCERNED CITIZEN.
SHOW YOUR SUPPORT FOR YOUR COUNTRY IN A
    RALLY.
10 AM, MARTYRS' SQUARE.
ALL SCHOOLS AND GOVERNMENT OFFICES CLOSED
    UNTIL AFTERNOON.

At Madame's, we watched the rallies from the window, and everyone wanted the best view. There was music and drumming. Dounia opened the window and almost hit Abudi in the head, which made him cry, even though he was nine, a big boy. Then Dounia almost cried, because she was so excited by the rallies.

There were men on the sidewalk, and the Quran playing. It

blasted from boom boxes the men carried. Next, women came
with their purses neatly on their arms and their good clothes on.
They marched, arms linked, in simple scarves and low heels for a
few minutes, before skipping out to go shopping. All the stores
were open. The police had not blocked off the street. As people
marched, they skipped between cars, flags sagging, and the buses
were all diverted to bring people into the rallies, not out the other
direction: these rallies were mandatory. You couldn't be seen on
your balcony, it meant you weren't at the rally.

Madame's children wanted to join the rally. All their school friends
were going. You could tell the schoolchildren in the crowd by their
blue and pink shirts like bubble gum under gray uniforms.

I, too, wanted to join the rallies. I was excited, like the children. I listened and moved to the beat of drumming and dancing.

Baba was not watching the rallies; he was praying in the living
room. His low chants mixed with the muted sound of rally slogans:
God All-Knowing, in God's name.

At Madame's, we didn't go down to the rallies, but we watched
them all the way up the street, and we followed them on TV.

Baba finished his prayers and sat down on the sofa between
Lema and me. He made contented sounds at us, like a dove cooing.

"How does a dove coo in English, Bea?"

Madame came in. She sighed into a chair and smiled at us.

"Ooli, Beatrice. Didn't they teach you in America not to lie on sofas with strange men?"

"That girl's my daughter."

"No, she's not."

"I love her like one. OK, Lema-Baba, where were we?"

He began to talk about revolution. Madame hummed softly beneath his voice.

"The situation here is very hard," Baba said. "You see these rallies? They mean the government is worried. When the government is worried, you never know what will happen. There are times the police want me, I go out with my hands crossed before me. I give them my passport. Take me."

It was very brave of him. In America, I never heard about policemen who came to get you for talking. My father and my friends' fathers never mentioned arrest as a normal thing, while their wives hummed softly, and after they'd just made sounds like doves cooing.

I sat on the sofa, feeling the adrenaline of revolution. It came in small acts with big meanings: people who broke small rules like driving Amo Nasir, the Nelson Mandela of this country, in their car. People who went to jail for little things, indiscretions. In this country, there was no habeas corpus. If the government decided you were a threat, then you could go to jail for years without knowing why, and without a trial. Baba had once been jailed that way. Here, it took big minds to commit indiscretions.

The resistance wasn't made up only of young boys, but old men. Old men who smoked in cars and grew wise, and sometimes let their wives and children care about the money and the work and their meals. Old men with children and wives like Amo Nasir's wife, Moni, and Madame, who never cared very much about resisting, but was resigned to it.

Recently, Baba and his friends had begun to talk about a new plan. They were frustrated with the government, which often threatened them and was occupying the neighboring country. This country's government did not allow free speech, but Baba and his friends had taken their frustrations and were in the process of writing them all down in a brave document calling for an end to censorship, and free elections. When it was done, they would publish this document, and each man would have to make his own decision about whether to sign it.

This put Baba in a dilemma. He believed in the document and wanted to sign, but he worried for Madame and the children.

The men were only writing their thoughts; they were not taking up arms, or plotting to overthrow the government. Still, here writing could be dangerous.

I heard Baba discussing it with Madame at night.

"Don't sign, Hassan," she told him. "What would we do without you?"

"I can't be a coward."

"Yes, but think of the children. What would happen to us, if you were gone?"

Now, on the sofa, Lema said, "I want the people I love close to me."

Baba said, "That's not real love. Look at the Americans. They love, but they say, Go. Go far away, and I'll call you and I'll love you, but I let you go."

"The Americans don't love the way we do."

"But they do, Lema-Baba, they do. Would you rather I locked you in a closet to show you I love you? Your problem is you're young. Look at Bea, how much she sometimes cries, I miss Mama, I miss America. Look at Nisrine. I would cry, too, if I were Nisrine's age. But now if I left tomorrow, I wouldn't cry. I wouldn't even call you, maybe."

"Why not?"

"Because I am grown now. I don't think with my emotions, I think with my mind."

I had only been at Madame's a little while, but I knew the person who cried most in our apartment wasn't Nisrine or me, it was Lema, because she was a teenager and going through a phase.

Whenever I thought of crying, I thought of the astonishing text in the National Library. The text told the story of Qais and Leila, a legend that could be found in other books, too, but my professors always said the familiar content didn't matter, that it was the words themselves that gave this text its unique beauty. I imagined astonishing words spread out before me. I imagined crying, for a single word's beauty.

Here, when you loved someone, you called her by your name.

On the sofa, Baba chucked Lema under her chin. "What I want for you, Lema-Baba, is not to be a number. There are not one hundred bookbinders in this country, there are ninety-nine and Hassan, you understand?"

Lema's father called her Baba, which was his name, and it showed he loved her like he loved himself. She was part of him as his own name.

JUST BEFORE BED, there was a phone call. Baba picked it up and stood for a moment, listening, then he went into the bedroom. We could hear him through the wall.

"They took Nasir."

"They took him?"

But we couldn't hear his answer.

Madame said, "I'll go see his wife tomorrow."

Baba came back into the living room, having changed out of his pajamas.

Madame said, "Nisrine, go fill up the water bottles."

So Nisrine, Lema, and I filled up the bottles before our water cut off for the night.

Baba had his shoes on, ready to go. Nisrine served him water from a bottle we'd filled. Then he bent to kiss each of us once and went out into the city. The air was hoarse with winter stoves, and the dusky, moonlit sky the same flat gray as cement.

We sat up for a while waiting. When Baba didn't return, Madame locked the door and took the children to bed. Nisrine poured milk in a cup for Dounia to drink before she slept, but Dounia didn't want to. She held the small layer of fat around Nisrine's waist and sucked it like a breast.

"Booby."

"My Dounia," Nisrine said. "My baby, my baby, my baby." She took a teaspoon and fed Dounia the milk. "One gulp, one suck, Dounia. One gulp, one suck."

Madame came in. She said, "Nisrine, you're spoiling her."

We carried Dounia to bed. Nisrine took her hands, I took her feet to swing her, in fun.

Abudi was already tucked in. He filled the room with the soft smell of sleeping.

"Booby."

Because it was late, there was no noise outside on the street. We listened a moment for a car, but there was none.

Nisrine had mostly forgiven me for her hair, but there was still sometimes a strangeness between us.

I wanted to ask if she was worried about Baba.

She cuddled Dounia. When the little girl wouldn't go to sleep, Nisrine cooed, and told her a story. It was about the young heroine who could change into a bird.

By now, Dounia knew this story. "Tell me a different one."

"A different one?" Nisrine thought for a moment. Then, she said, "We had trouble in Indonesia when I was young, just like here. We had car bombs, too. And riots in the streets. One day, I woke up and our door was burned down."

"What did you do?"

"My father is a smart man. Like our Baba here, he's very

intellectual. He went out and bought my mother flowers. He told me don't tell, it was his surprise. When he got home, my mother was sleeping. He snuck them through that burned door and put them in her wedding vase on the table, then he went to take a nap. My mother woke up and she didn't see them. She made dinner in the kitchen. She read on the front steps. My father woke up and she still didn't see them, until she set the table. 'Oh, there're flowers here. Who did that?' My father was in the bedroom, but they were his flowers, so I didn't answer. My mother said, 'Nisrine, who put these flowers here?' Like he'd never done that before. My mother went to the bedroom. 'Salem, there're flowers on the table.' 'Well, yeah,' my father said. My father is like that."

I imagined Nisrine: young, with a vase of flowers, an accomplice to her father.

Dounia didn't understand. "Why did he buy flowers?"

"To give us something to love," Nisrine told her. "He knew, even with a burned door, if he bought flowers we would have something growing. It's important to have that. Within you, too. That's why, here, I'm still trying to grow my heart." She gave a little laugh.

"Isn't your heart big enough already?"

"No, it won't grow. I keep trying. I need something to ground it."

"Like what?"

"A plant." She laughed again. "My father's flowers. Or, a man. Something to care for."

I asked, "What about Dounia?"

"I care for Dounia, don't I, Dounia?"

Dounia was almost asleep. Nisrine quietly kissed her.

What about her husband?

This question went unasked, and unanswered.

But, as if Nisrine could read my thoughts, she said, "You know my husband has funny feet? I remember when we were married, we both sat on the lap of my father; I looked down from my father's knee, and I saw my husband's feet stuck out in a funny position. I asked, 'Were your feet always like that?' I had been so busy looking in his face, I never noticed them before."

"Blinded by love!" I joked, which was sometimes how my mother explained the years she spent with my father.

Nisrine shrugged. She had loved her husband from a look. She was a maid in a house, he came to deliver a package. She saw him at the door and knew he was her fate, so she looked at him, and he loved her. Though, later there were problems.

"You loved just from a look?" I'd asked when she first told me.

I had never met anyone who loved just from a look.

I had read stories about heroines who loved that way.

I looked out at the police station.

Nisrine sighed. "I miss love, Bea. It's good to love, it makes you feel a part of something."

I had never been in love. I had liked men, but the ones I liked didn't always like me. I sat on the bed and thought about this fact, and about Nisrine, far away from her husband, in a house working for revolution, trying to grow her heart. I thought it had to do with how much she missed home; trying to miss it less, and care about here more. That way, she wouldn't lose a sense of herself while she was away. Like me, I thought, Nisrine wanted to feel deeply.

"Nisrine, how do you grow your heart?"

"I don't know."

In the dark bedroom, she and I both leaned against the head-board, feeling for our hearts. Then, Nisrine took my hand and put it over hers.

"I can't feel it, can you?"

So, through her hand and her chest, I felt for Nisrine's heart. It was true, the beat was hard to find. We both knew it was there.

"It's because here is so small, every day is the same."

"Do you think you'll find a way to grow it?"

"I don't know, I hope so. I have to, to want to stay."

I hoped so, too. Nisrine had a contract; it seemed to me, she had little choice in when to leave, and she was saving up money to send her child, and for a house. Still, I hoped she and I would both find reasons to stay, and large hearts.

IN THE MORNING, Baba was still gone, and so the walls of the apartment closed in on us, one by one. First it was the fake window in the bathroom. There were no windows in the bathroom, but we'd hung a curtain over the water stain to pretend. First that got to us. Then slowly the ceiling and the squat door frames, until we smirked sourly like Nisrine smirked when she was mad at Madame, as if at our own terrible, private joke that was not at all funny but we laughed anyway, until finally after breakfast we really laughed, because Baba came home.

A GROWING HEART. I set out to find a way to grow my heart; that is, to feel more, and to find more things to love.

I looked for this first in the small things. I took time to appreciate the Milo we drank in the mornings, the richness of the chocolate and cream.

But, though I tried this, Baba's late nights got in the way of the Milo, for me.

Living here, there were certain things you learned about dictatorship. Everyone knew that the only newspaper was the government's newspaper, and the only telephone company was the government's company, as well as the bus company and the oil company. Even the language school was government run. I was not to say anything bad about the president to our neighbors, or the bus drivers, or the phone operators, because they all worked for the president, who was the former president's son.

There was only so much you could say under a dictatorship, and so there was lots of silence, and that was why the TV was always on. The president's picture was in every shop, and on our mantel, and all the billboards. Sometimes a policeman followed me when I was walking because I was foreign, but it didn't matter because danger came in talking, not walking, and so if I was silent, then he was my safety. I could walk past large groups of men at three a.m. and it wouldn't matter because he was there, and he was always watching. I learned that here there was no Facebook or YouTube, and that if we got Facebook or YouTube (as in the past few years this country had gotten cell phones and Internet), then it would be because the government had found a way to monitor Facebook (as it monitored my Internet), and so I must not post provocative statements about the depressed economy. I learned that the walls had ears, and so did the neighbors, and because I was foreign, I was especially suspect, so I must compensate by always saying how much I loved this country, and the neighbors would compensate by always trying to engage me to their sons for citizenship, and I should never, ever tell them that I was scared because Amo Nasir gave an interview and now he was in jail, and there'd been talk of a secret document, and phone calls in the night, and these things were small, but we felt their danger. Baba left without telling us where he was going, or when he would return.

Madame said, "Bea needs something to do. She's restless because she's bored."

And she gave me the chicken to clean.

I stood in the kitchen, peeling away the skin of the chicken in small pieces, while Lema held back my bangs so I could see. Lema said, "Bea wants to study. The university still hasn't called her."

Madame said, "You want to study, Bea? I'll be your tutor. I correct you all the time. You should be paying me!"

I said, "No, thank you. I'll find my own tutor."

But Madame called up Baba anyway, to ask him for suggestions.

On the phone, Baba thought this request was very funny. He joked, "I hear Arabic tutors have many girlfriends."

Madame said, "What's the matter with that, dear?"

"I mean girlfriends in the English sense, dear."

But, he promised to look for me.

In the meantime, Madame sent me out to the National Library for a second try, just to see.

She said, "Come back soon, Bea. If you come back in the afternoon, I might fall asleep, and then you'll be stuck, who'll open the door?"

I walked along streets littered with paper and lost shoes from the rallies.

At the library, the same woman behind the desk greeted me. I was trying to grow my heart, so I said hello very nicely, and wrote down a request for the astonishing text. Then, I got out a book from my purse so I could read while I waited, but the librarian stopped me.

"No outside books."

"This is a library. It's a place for books."

"Not in the waiting area." She meant the cage.

"Then what will I do while I wait?"

"You can recite books."

Here, children memorized books. Girls Dounia's age could recite the whole Quran.

I hadn't memorized any books. The librarian was surprised.

"None?" She didn't know what to do about this. "Then use your imagination. You must have an imagination, you read."

I waited in the cage all day without a book, trying to use my imagination. At the end of the day, the librarian came to the cage, empty-handed, to let the scholars and me out.

When I got home, Madame was disappointed: a second time failed.

"Did you flirt, Bea? Did you give them a gift?"

"No."

She shook her head. "What did you expect, that they'd give you a book for free?"

I hadn't heard from the university, and I was having trouble with the library.

So instead, Madame sent me down to the garden with Dounia and Abudi. We could see from the window the garden was almost empty, that was why she let us go. "Don't talk to anyone," she said, because of Baba's revolution, while we waited for the elevator, which was slow and crippled and wheezing without a door so you could see the cement walls and each floor as you went down. "Don't tell anyone where we live. Come back up right away if there are too many children."

There was only a woman and her little girl in the garden. Dounia and Abudi ran around the swing set at once, brushing the dirt off the seats. Then they each took a swing, and began twisting.

The other little girl took the swing between them and said hello. Dounia and Abudi looked at me. We weren't supposed to talk to anyone. They all swung around some more, on their bellies. They twisted and untwisted in a line, facing me.

The other little girl said, "What's your name?"

Abudi looked at me. I didn't say anything. I took out my book, and began to read.

"What's their name?" the little girl asked.

I said, "Abudi."

She said, "Abudi."

Abudi looked at me.

They all swung in a row, facing out. The little girl asked, "How old are you?" They were all between four and nine. Dounia asked, "Is your mom veiled?" The little girl said yes, she's over there. No one looked where she'd pointed, they all faced out, toward me. In the margins of my book, I doodled Arabic. I made a perfect *B*.

Dounia said, "Who'll play on the slide with me?"

All three of them ran over to the slide. Instead of sliding, they picked up used straws. I told them not to put those in their mouths. They told me they'd only draw with them. I said those are very dirty. They put them down. They picked them up again. I said, if they were going to play like that, we'd have to leave. I hoped Madame wasn't watching from the window, because we still weren't supposed to talk to anyone, and Dounia was going to tell for sure that we played with straws and talked to a little girl, but then a man's voice came from behind me.

"Don't play with those, baba, give them to me."

I turned around.

It was Adel, the blond policeman.

I felt a warming in my stomach and my knees.

He walked over to the sandbox and collected the children's straws, firmly. Then he turned and dropped them in my lap.

"We don't let children play with straws here," he said, "they're dirty."

Adel stood at the bench looking down, very close to me. The only time we'd been closer was when Nisrine and I gave him apples. His leather jacket was open to a vest with brass stars. Underneath, he wore a white T-shirt, like the ones Abudi wore at night to sleep. A single blond curl peeked out from the shirt's neck.

He was looking at my book, which was still open in my lap.

"Where are you from?" he asked. "America?"

"Yes, America."

The children clumped to one side of the sandbox to watch us. They sat with their bodies facing the street and their mouths open.

Adel said, "I have a cousin in Wisconsin. You know Wisconsin?"

We weren't supposed to talk to anyone. I was trying hard not to talk to him, but everything he said made me want to agree. Like he had just asked me out to a movie, or Friday night coffee—

"Yes, Wisconsin," I said, trying to look serious for the children.

"You might be neighbors."

I had never been to Wisconsin.

"Yes, we might!" I agreed.

The policeman smiled down at me. He had little dimples in his cheeks, like stars.

"What's your name?"

"Bea."

"You write Arabic, Bea? I've never met an American who writes Arabic."

In their box, the children ran their fingers through the sand, bunching it up, letting it fall from their fists like rain.

Adel sat down on the bench beside me.

"I write, too," he said. "I write poetry."

"You do?"

He took my book, turned the page, and wrote a word down in the margin.

"This is what I write for the girl I love, do you know it?"

Later, I would know this word. I would know that it was often used in poems in the Middle Ages, and it comes from the root *ayn-sheen-qaf,* which means the deepest feeling.

I didn't know it then.

Adel told me, "It means a poet's love."

I couldn't believe my luck. Here I was, trying to mind Madame's children, and suddenly I was talking about love with the blond policeman. I thought of Nisrine, whose husband had loved her with a look. I tried to look at Adel; his face was wide and sunny, it burned a hole right through my chest. So, I looked instead at the word he'd written. Its letters lined up soft and full by the printed page. They curved close to one another, like an embrace.

I didn't know where to look after that thought.

I said, "Your writing is very pretty."

"It's pretty? Your eyes are the pretty. The Arabic language is very deep, there are ninty-nine words for love alone in Arabic, did you know that?"

I felt my red cheeks.

Adel didn't seem to notice. He wrote another word in the margin, then he took out a piece of paper from his pocket. On it was a verse of poetry.

"Can you read it?" he asked.

Carefully, I took the paper from him.

To My Flower, the Jasmine, it read. *Peace to the one with hair like dusk falling. Even her Sweat smells Sweet.*

"Can you guess who it's about?" Adel asked.

There was a strange feeling in my throat.

"A girl with dark hair?"

I had light hair—

But before Adel could answer, we heard a shout from above.

"Bea! Abudi!" It was Madame. She had seen the children playing with straws, and she had seen me talking to the policeman.

I stood up. "I have to go."

Adel stood up, too. "It was nice to meet you, Bea." He held out his hand and for a moment our fingers touched, and then the children and I were running away across the street.

. . .

In the elevator on the way up, the children and I were giddy. We shared our recklessness in talking to a policeman and sucking on used straws, two great secrets. Abudi said, "Bea, Dounia used to be scared to go up the elevator alone. She used to be too small to reach the buttons."

There was sand everywhere, on all of us, and I was trying to brush it off. I turned Dounia around to brush her backside. I ran my fingers through my hair and the pages of my book, and the paper with the policeman's poem fell out.

Abudi stopped me.

"What's that?"

I picked it up. In my rush, I'd forgotten to give it back to him. For a moment, my finger lingered over the letters.

This is what I write for the girl I love.

"Nothing." We were already in trouble. I searched my pocket for change. "Here, Abudi. Don't tell your mother. Get yourself a treat."

MY SECRET POEM.

It stayed all day in my pocket, while Madame looked us over and pronounced us dusty; while we rolled up our pant legs and our sleeves, and trooped carefully through the clean house so Nisrine could help us wash on the balcony.

In the evening, while the children got ready for bed, I helped

Nisrine dry the dishes, and afterwards, I slipped out the poem, smoothed it across my leg like he had, and laid it before her.

"What's this, Bea?"

We both bent over it. Nisrine reached out to trace the letters. I reached with her. There was something about the poem that made you want to touch it.

"It's pretty," she said. The paper was thin and gauzy. When we held it up to the light, it glowed. "It's beautiful."

I thought so, too.

"It's special. Who wrote it?"

There was a noise behind us. Lema came in. Nisrine had been holding the poem. She handed it to me, and I tried to slip it quickly under a dish towel, but it was too late. Lema had already seen it.

"What's that, Bea?"

Reluctantly, I held it out for her. There was a smudge of ink in one corner, and I dabbed it carefully with my finger. Lema leaned on my shoulder and read the poem out loud, while we listened.

"'To my flower, the jasmine. Peace to the one with hair like dusk falling.'"

"It's pretty," she said. "Where did you find it?"

I was hesitant. "The garden."

"Look at its perfect letters. The poet's quite a Qais." Meaning, it was a deep poem. Lema continued reading. "'Even her sweat smells sweet.'" She looked up. "That's strange. No girl's sweat smells sweet."

At Madame's, we all used the same deodorant, so we all smelled the same: the first days after our baths, we were sweet; after that, we became stinky. When I lifted my arms before the mirror, I could see salty half-moon marks, which were the same marks I saw on Nisrine's pajama shirts and I had begun to see on Lema's dirty bras. This was how I knew Lema was growing. She was no longer a flat line beside me beneath the covers at night; she grew round, her hips stuck out.

In Arabic, the word for a woman's sweat is *arak*, from the root *ayn-ra-qaf*, which is also the name of a liquor made from dates or anise seed. The date liquor is bitter. It's clear like sweat, but burns when you swallow.

Baba kept a bottle of arak behind his fresh-bound books in the closet. He used it in his factory, to warm his men in winter. They took small sips from porcelain cups, like tea.

Baba once gave me some arak as a joke, and laughed when I coughed. Now, I could still call up the burning feeling; it pierced and pulsed like the poem did, *arak*, *arak*—or, like Adel did, a warm insistence that spread through my limbs like sun.

Lema traced the letters. "Do you think it's about Nisrine?" she asked.

I had been thinking about *arak*. I thought I hadn't heard Lema.

"What?"

Lema said, "'Hair like dusk falling.' Nisrine has dark hair."

I glanced at Nisrine. Her eyes were very bright. Her hand rose absently to her veil, and then she remembered. And I remembered. The flat back of her veil, where her bun used to be.

There was a moment of silence, while I tried not to care that Nisrine had dusk hair, and she seemed to be trying not to care that I had cut it.

The moment passed.

Lema handed the poem back to me.

I couldn't stop looking at Nisrine's bright eyes, which would not meet mine; they followed the poem.

Reluctantly, I waved it toward her. "Do you still want to see this?"

"No, you can keep it."

So, I put it away in my book.

Madame came in and said it was time for bed.

After we brushed our teeth, I lay beside Lema, her leg against my leg, my arm up against her arm, thinking.

"Bea," she asked, "what do you know about men?"

I didn't know much. When I imagined having a boyfriend, I had always imagined someone who knew both *Jane Eyre* and Ibn 'Arabi.

Lema said, "I had a boyfriend once."

"You did?"

"Yes, he was very sweet, he got me a stuffed soccer ball with a heart sewed on it. I had to lie to my mother about where I found it. He broke up with me, though, when he found out who my father is."

She meant when he found out her father worked for revolution.

I said, "I think your father is very brave."

"He is," Lema said. She paused. The station lights came through the window. "Sometimes, though, I don't want a brave father. Sometimes, I'd rather have a boyfriend."

I THOUGHT ABOUT THE POEM, and wondered who it was for, and carried it around in my pocket, but I found no more chances for conversation with the blond policeman, and I had no new ideas about the dusk-haired girl.

We still weren't supposed to talk to anyone. Baba worked for revolution. There was trouble on the streets.

But it was hard not to talk. Everyone was curious about Americans and I didn't want to be impolite, so I talked with a neighbor in the elevator who wanted to engage me to her eldest son.

"Where do you live?" she asked.

I pushed the fifth-floor button. I said in perfect Arabic, "Madame's."

An hour later, the woman knocked on our door. She'd brought her son.

I hid in the bedroom.

"American?"

Even Nisrine was scandalized. "Bea, mothers-in-law won't bring you love."

In the hall, we could hear Madame. "Shoo, get out. She doesn't want to marry you. Go on."

. . .

After that, I wasn't allowed to tell people I lived at Madame's.

"They're nosey. They don't need to know. If they ask, tell them you're a governess."

"A governess?"

"But you leave at night, you don't stay."

"So, where do I live?"

Madame looked at me, exasperated. "For God's sake, Bea. You're American. Tell them you live alone."

There was a list of things I wasn't allowed to do:

Go down to the garden with the children. I might come back married.

Do my own laundry; I mixed the whites with the colors and turned my sweater pink.

Stay out late.

Wear my shoes on the carpet.

Say the word "God" in the bathroom.

Play with the children when they should go to bed.

Wear the traditional scarf for men.

Drink from Abudi's purple cup.

WHEN I FIRST CAME TO THIS CITY, it was all in color. The green points of the mosques at night, the bright seeds of the pomegranates that Nisrine split and peeled like rubies for me to eat. This city seemed to me like Arabic; how many words I learned, those were all the shades of color I could see.

After the colors, though, I began to see the dirt. It was wedged between my fingernails, gray and muted green.

I began to feel dirt, caught between my teeth with the pomegranate seeds.

In my American college, I had learned to be thoughtful and value good scholarship. I knew how to read a work of literature and isolate a theme, and I thought one way of becoming wise could be by reading books.

When I first arrived at Madame's, I had thought that my long days in the house would be temporary. I planned to gain a university and a tutor, and eventually to read the astonishing text.

Of course, I was beginning to realize that what had seemed like simple goals were actually quite difficult. Even for citizens, this country did not work quickly. I thought of my friends in their college classes, the meaningful discussions they must be having.

At Madame's, I began to sneak small freedoms: Extra paper in the bathroom. A sip, when Madame wasn't looking, from Abudi's purple cup.

Nisrine had said, *It's good to love, it makes you feel a part of something.*

I had wanted to be a part.

But, the poem had brought back the strangeness between us.

To make up for cutting Nisrine's hair, I went out and bought two bottles of perfume, one for Madame, one for Nisrine. Madame took both of them. They were both the same size.

"Don't worry, Bea, I'll find something you can give her." And she rummaged in her closet for a cheaper gift to give me, to give Nisrine.

At the end of the month, there was a polite fight about paying rent.

"No no, I couldn't," Madame said.

"You must, you must."

"You're like family."

"You must, you must. I insist!"

I wanted to pay. With Madame, paying was how I still felt free.

ONCE A MONTH, I took out money from the American embassy, and when I did, I was supposed to bring back a bottle of whiskey for Baba and a box of Virginia Slims for Madame, from the embassy store. But then one day, before I could give Baba his whiskey, Madame took it and gave it to Nisrine, who hid it, and this was how I knew things had changed. Another of Baba's friends was taken and beaten. Baba called often now to tell us not to wait on him for dinner, he wouldn't be home.

We lay widthwise across the bed, talking.

Nisrine said, "I don't think Lema will ever marry. Husbands are too depressing."

Madame looked at her. "Nonsense, it's just my luck. Her luck will be better."

I asked, "Would you marry again, Nisrine?"

"I can't, I'm already married."

I was still making up to Nisrine. "Isn't he waiting for you?"

"Yes, he waits for me. He doesn't care for my child. My mama cares for my child."

Madame said, "That's just the way men are. They can't do the caring. They give you money."

I lay on the bed. So that I wouldn't worry about Baba, I concentrated on the blond policeman. How sweet his smile was with the dimples. How he had just met me, and talked to me immediately about poetry. How impressed he had been that I knew Arabic. I had always liked talking about poetry, in Arabic.

Beside me, I could feel Nisrine. Her hand rested against her chest like a small bird.

We were almost asleep when we heard a car oustide the apartment.

Madame said, "That's Hassan, I can feel it."

We opened the blinds and watched Baba get out of the car. He held a hand to his eyes, to shield them from the station's lights. We watched while he slowly made his way by himself in the dark night, the lights following him like animal eyes all the way up the curb, toward our house. When he entered our building, they slid away.

✹

THE NEXT MORNING, fear followed me. I worried about being arrested. I hid Adel's poem and wouldn't look at it, I was too worried about police. I worried just looking out our window at the billboards that held the leering face of the president.

At Madame's, whatever it was, I didn't want anything to do with it. About how Nisrine couldn't clean right, or Abudi wouldn't do his homework, or Baba's late nights. I was scared. I didn't want anything to do with them, so I closed the door to the bedroom. It was rude. I didn't care.

But the house was small, there were always policemen at the window, and children who wanted in. So, instead, I closed myself in the bathroom. The toilet would accept only certain things. Not paper, there was a basket for that. Not snot, you did that in your handkerchief. You could tell by the smells who'd been in. Nisrine had the smell of wet spinach.

Dounia turned the light off on me.

Lema said, "Mama! Look what your daughter is doing. Just look at her."

"Dounia! Naughty girl!" Madame knocked on the door. "Bea. You can hit her when you come out of the bathroom, and I won't say anything."

I came out of the bathroom.

"Go to sleep, Bea, you look tired."

"I'm not tired." But I went toward the bedroom.

Then Baba said, "Baba."

Silence.

He said again, "Baba."

Lema said, "Bea, he's calling you."

"Yes, Baba? You want something?"

"Nescafé."

"Nescafé."

So instead of the bedroom, I went to make Nescafé in the small kitchen. Nisrine was putting away the glasses and singing in English. She helped me to boil water.

"*My love is your love*," she sang.

When I returned with the Nescafé, Baba was still there on the sofa, one eye a half-moon, the other sleeping.

"Thank you, Baba," he said when I came in, and I realized he'd been calling me Baba like he did the children, and this is how I knew things really had changed. Abudi drove a tin truck beneath my feet. I held Lema's hand at night. I was part of a mother and a father and three children and a maid, and we all sat together at the dinner table and Dounia always wanted to tell a joke like Nisrine did, but it had no punch line, it was just another story, and we all washed our hands and then we ripped the flat bread into strips and used our fingers on the bread to pick up olives, except Lema, who got a bowl from the cupboard and a knife and fork to cut her meat because she was fourteen and going through a phase. And all of us were called Baba. As if we were one person with fourteen arms called Baba, as if there was no difference between us and Baba, and so, I must no longer linger in the garden and talk to strangers, I must stay at home with Madame, and if police came, I might be afraid, but I must sit still anyway until they were gone, because I was no longer free, even if I was American.

I liked a blond policeman. Sometimes, I imagined he was Qais, and I was Leila. I had cut a maid's hair. But, I was a young woman called Baba. And I had no choice, anymore, but to be on the side of this family.

HOME

SOMETHING MOST AMERICANS don't understand is how to learn a new language, you have to surrender. In Arabic, there were not only new words, but a new alphabet, and new sounds. My throat and tongue felt different speaking it. I had to retrain not only my mind, but my body, and in doing this, I had to let go of the logic I used in English. Like a child, my tongue felt heavy until I learned again to speak with it. But eventually, this surrender became what I loved. I pronounced letters that most Americans didn't dream existed. The rasping *kha*, like falling gravel, the *sad*, like a windy boat. I gave in to these new sounds; and giving in, I set my tongue free.

Like learning to speak, part of living at Madame's meant giving up certain routines. We drank coffee late at night, here. I was used to being independent, but Madame laid out my clothes in the morning. We worried about oil, each plate had its own separate sponge.

When I wrote this to a friend in America, she wrote me back: *Doesn't it bother you, you're like a child? You're twenty-one, what if you want to bring a man home? Go out and explore!*

But, I *was* exploring, just not the way my friend imagined.

Each day at Madame's, new words unfurled before me. I wrote them down in a little notebook, and in the evenings I went through them, memorizing them one by one, imagining them as they might appear in the astonishing text. Sometimes, Nisrine helped me.

I remembered the excitement of my first texts in Arabic, how even simple words opened worlds for me. I imagined fluency, like jasmine flowers from the policeman's poem, in bloom after a long rain.

Of course, I cared about being twenty-one and grown up and independent. But I liked living at Madame's.

For the first time, I was part of a large family. For an only child, sometimes this can be enough.

Like Arabic, which I first loved through surrender, I was beginning to see how dependence could be a form of learning. Learning is a form of being free.

BEFORE MADAME, Baba had a different wife and a different family. They lived with him in the same rooms full of sunlight that we lived in and, unlike Lema, their firstborn was a son. He was born just a few years before I was.

In the 1980s, when his son was two, Baba was put in jail. Some men came to his factory where he bound Qurans. They took him in their car, and one of the men slowly forced Baba's head down into another man's lap so he couldn't see, and when Baba returned from jail ten years later, he didn't have a family anymore. He'd only been two miles away, underground, but no one knew this, even him, and now his brother ran his factory—he didn't have that either—and his wife had given him up for gone and loved another man, so he had to start from scratch. But he had a house, and he had resistance.

When I thought too much about Baba I got sentimental, and I began to see jail as the answer to all my questions. It was why Baba's hands looked very old around the knuckles and why, when he prayed, we saw the withered bottoms of his feet; they'd withered up from the beatings in jail.

Baba liked food. He bought the best food for our apartment, and a computer with a big screen. There was a large window in his kitchen that he could look out—in jail there was no window, just a lightbulb, when it was on that was day, when it was off that was night—and he had three new, healthy, post-jail children and Madame, his wife, and he built all this. All this was his to be proud of.

I was learning to live with Baba's resistance; to accept fear in the background, a dull thrum.

Still, I worried, especially when I remembered his secret free elections document. It was such a small thing, to write down some complaints and sign them. It seemed unfair that it could lead to so much trouble. If only I had known what was to come.

Baba had lived with the police a long time now. For more than thirty years (ten of those in jail) he had worked for the resistance, and he did this the whole time living beside the Central Police Station.

I thought back to how Lema and I had played prettiest policeman, and I'd only liked the blond one, but when Baba had found out, instead of being mad, he laughed. How can you laugh when a woman like your daughter picks a favorite from among the police? But maybe Baba's reaction said something about how adaptable we are as humans. When we must, we can get used to almost anything. Like Nisrine, who didn't talk to me at first after I cut her hair, and who hadn't left the house except once to get groceries. But if she minded, she didn't show it. She kept trying to grow her heart. She beat the rugs in the morning. She sang in the kitchen and made faces at Dounia.

Maybe adaptability is a form of bravery.

YOU MAY HAVE ALREADY GUESSED who the blond policeman loved, but I was still unsure. There were many dark-haired women in this city. I kept his poem, an intimate kind of mystery that we didn't talk about.

As the days passed we adapted to this, like so much else.

I wondered, though, and I dreamed.

Some nights, restless, I rose, untangled myself from Lema, and moved silent as dust past Nisrine and the sleeping children to the kitchen, where I indulged in feeling alone. I sat still with my head on the table. I kept the lights off.

The city was unrecognizable at night. Looking out, all I could see was black; the dark monuments to the president, the unlit hole of our garden where, one night, I thought I could see Adel standing—deep in the darkness of our garden, bending and straightening: Was he searching for something? Was he restless, like me?

Now I know why he was searching. I didn't then, but my heart went out to him: a man alone, savoring his aloneness, like me.

Our garden was our scrapbook; it could tell you everything. All along its paths were small traces of life at Madame's and the station: orange peels, smoked cigarette butts, stray strands of Nisrine's cut hair. It had been a long time now and I wanted to forget, but her hair lingered. We kept finding it in unlikely places—a rung of the swing set, a swallow's nest the children found, wrapped around a stray cat's tail.

Beside Nisrine's hair, the jasmine also bloomed along the bushes and the fence of the garden. The flowers bent, small and bone white, their perfume evaporating up into the night, over our balcony, and into the stars, where if there had been a light I would have seen it, the way Adel combed carefully through the bushes, hand on each leaf until finally when he straightened—a dark line like dusk, the night sky like smoke—he held a strand of Nisrine's stray hair.

It was night, and I was too far away.

What I saw was the man, his long shape and bare head in the moonlight. Later, his movements took on a sudden lightness. He lifted his arm, looked at his finger, and my heart, too, went up in gladness that whatever he was searching for, he'd found.

WHEN WEEKS PASSED and I still hadn't heard from the university, Baba called a friend, and his friend found a tutor for me. My tutor had studied in London for one year and now he had lots of students, so he was used to foreigners. On the phone before we met, he said his name was Imad but his London friends called him Matt to show affection, which Madame thought was funny.

"Matt?" she said. The word *mat* meant dead in Arabic.

"Matt."

"Matt *mat*, *Allah yerhamo*." It was what you said when someone died: *Allah yerhamo*. God rest him. Madame shook her head. "Bea, you in the West have strange signs of affection."

. . .

Before my first lesson, there was a rush to get ready, and the family helped me. Nisrine ran a lint roller across my jeans. Lema lent me a necklace of red beads.

Madame stood in the doorway, skeptical. "Don't tell him anything, Bea. To be a tutor you need a license. That means he talks to the government."

She made me turn around so she could see that my shirt covered the top of my jeans.

The first time I met Imad, he wore a burgundy vest and had chapped lips that he said came from the salt in the ocean. His parents were from a beach town. In class, it was only Maria from Spain and me, and we each had a different vocabulary. I told Imad that someday I wanted to read the astonishing text in the National Library, and he told me he could help; he would teach me classical poetry.

That day, to start, we read a poem and made up similes. Maria was being gregarious. She described her hands as hard like amethysts. I described my eyes as round like lentils, which made Imad laugh.

Maria said to him, "Ooh, is that cashmere?"

Imad said yes.

"Ooh, can I touch it?"

So Maria and I both touched Imad's burgundy vest across the table.

"Very nice," Maria said, "very nice."

"It's vintage," said Imad.

I was also being gregarious, but without trying. I was wearing the red necklace from Lema. For conversation practice, Maria told a story about a pointy pair of Egyptian shoes that a car ran over. She meant the car ran over her toe—or the pointy part of the shoes. In Maria's stories, it seemed, it was always important to note what she was wearing. When it was my turn, I told a story about how I dropped a pickle glass on my toe when I was in high school, and it broke my toe but not the glass.

Imad leaned over to correct me. "We say jar, not glass, Bea." But, he said it nicely.

On my way back to Madame's, everything felt light and giddy. Lema opened the door for me.

"What's with all the prettiness, Bea?" She made me turn around once, and called her mother to come look. "Uh-huh, see what one necklace does? Now you look like a girl."

It was the day my mother was supposed to call from America. On the phone, I could not stop babbling, and imposing the best of this country's wisdom.

"Here, we make tea with cardamom," I said. "Have you ever tried tea with cardamom?"

"Here, we never eat on the run. Are you eating on the run, Mom? You should let it digest."

I was enjoying being generous.

"How much is this phone call? You want to hang up and I'll call you back?"

On the other end, I could imagine exactly how my mother stood in the door the way she had always stood, the way her mother must have stood, because we all stood that way—my mother, my aunts, me: head and stomach forward, neck and shoulders curled into the back making the shape of a clamshell. Her arm drew imperfect angles at her hip; her hand rested against her elbow. My mother said, "Don't turn Arab on me, Bea."

THERE WERE NO BIRDS IN THIS CITY, only the doves that the mosques let out in the evening to fly overhead, and remind us the sky was empty when they were gone. They floated in lazy circles above the slate rooftops, their wings like sooty fingerprints on the clean-swept sky. We lived near a mosque, so we always saw the birds from a distance, as small blots on our horizon. They had been let out now and circled above us, proclaiming their absence. Blown by the small winds, they swept low over the police station, where a blond man stood on the rooftop, waving.

Abudi flew a plastic-bag kite off the balcony.

"Look, Bea, it's a bird!"

"It's a kite."

"It's a fish!"

The kite flew with the other doves, trying to catch them. The wind rustled the trees. The kite dipped and veered into the garden, where it caught in the bushes.

Nisrine and I came running. "Abudi, your kite!"

"It's not a kite, it's a fish!"

"It's not a fish, it's a heart!"

"A broken heart!"

We pulled the bag up. It came away in two pieces, unhinged. Abudi took them both and ran inside.

The blond policeman was still waving.

Nisrine and I stood on the balcony. When Abudi had gone, Nisrine brought a rug to shake.

He was still waving.

I waved back to him, but he didn't seem to notice.

Nisrine beat the rug.

Waving, and waving.

She hung it over the balcony rail and squinted out at the policeman, who was watching. He had spent months, waiting.

Finally, she sighed and pointed to herself. "Is he waving at me?" Her finger touched her heart and as suddenly as it had begun, the waving stopped. He stood very still in the setting sun, hair shining. Slowly, while I watched, his hand slid down from his wave, over his shoulder, onto his heart. And, if there was strangeness left between us, then this is how Nisrine and I finally, really made up.

She turned to me. "You don't mind, do you, Bea?"

I minded. I was trying not to mind.

Her eyes were shining.

"No."

She said, "Don't tell anyone."

Nisrine was a maid who wanted to grow her heart, so she wouldn't miss home. I was a student who wanted to read a text, who wanted to grow my heart, too, who wanted to feel, deeply.

I had cut Nisrine's hair, but she had no choice now, except to trust me. And I had no choice now, except not to mind. Because, even though I had liked him first, we both knew who the policeman's poem was about.

Adel was touching his heart.

Nisrine was touching her heart.

She put a hand on my hand like she'd done once before, and put it over her heart, to show me—"Can you feel it, Bea?"

It had begun to grow.

LOVE BEGINS

(RECONSTRUCTED WITH THE
HELP OF ADEL'S LETTERS)

ADEL CALLED AGAIN AND AGAIN to the house phone while Madame was out.

Nisrine played coy.

"Hello, dear, how are you?"

"Fine." (Giggling.)

"Where are you? I miss you!"

She looked at me. "With people."

"When can I see you?"

"I don't know. Maybe later."

She took the children down to play in the garden, where Adel was waiting. Madame could see from the window it was empty except for a policeman, that was why she let them go. "Don't talk to anyone," she said, as she always did. "Come back up if there are too many children."

But there was just a blond policeman, who took a seat on a bench facing Nisrine. A wisp of hair had escaped from under her white veil, and he wanted to touch it. So he said instead, "Why don't you straighten your hair?"

"I don't like to, you like it better straight?"

"Honestly, Nisrine, from the moment I saw you I loved you."

They were two heads, close together by the bushes.

The children ran around the swing set once. Above them, Madame and I at the window were watching.

"How old are you?" Nisrine asked.

"How old do you think?"

"Don't lie."

"Nisrine, I love you. I wouldn't lie."

"Then, how old are you?"

"How old are you?"

"I asked first."

"I'm twenty-one."

"You're lying."

"I'm not, do you want to see my identity card?"

"Yes."

"I don't have it with me."

She looked at him. Her eyes were clear and black, two sides of a dark desert.

"Fine, I'm twenty-three."

He laid his hand beside hers. Two years between them.

He said, "That's good, then."

. . .

They did not know where this left them. He watched her sweep, her heart-shaped butt.

He called again and again until Madame answered, then he hung up.

Later, Nisrine said, "Don't call me, silly, you'll get me in trouble!" Laughing.

They tried again, a second time in the garden. This time, Adel was ready.

"Nisrine, do you know the desert?"

She knew the desert.

"My grandfather is from there. He says there is one flower that is more beautiful than all the others, that blooms only once every hundred years. I think you might be that flower."

"I might?"

"I think so. My grandfather is an important man, he fought for the president. He was captured by the enemy."

She said, "My grandfather knew the ocean. He once beat back a flood with a stick."

He said, "Your grandfather had magical powers!"

She liked this. "Your grandfather sounds very brave."

They sat a moment in silence. That wisp of hair was blowing about her veil again, wanting him to touch it. He said instead, "That's good, then."

THERE IS A LANGUAGE that develops in love. When the circumstance is extreme (looking out from a roof, over a balcony, high above the world), then so can be the language. Theirs was of epic proportion.

They talked with their hands across the street and the garden. He stood on the rooftop, she on the balcony. Because they were far apart, it was a language of large movements. Of arms flung wide open, chests out, legs spread to express great meaning. Years later Adel would remember this, and it would still give him goose bumps, even after all that had happened.

She leaned over the balcony, palms up as if to catch him. He touched his eyes with a long arm. It meant, Anything you need, I'll give it to you. It meant, Even my eyes are yours alone, I've saved you even my eyes.

In the evening, Nisrine ironed with the blinds open. Dounia and Abudi played Let's Go Hajj by the table. They put a box in the center for the Kaaba stone. They ran around it seven times. They leaned their heads out the window to feel the desert, facing the mountain.

Nisrine took off her outer veil and laid it aside on the counter. She took off her inner veil and laid it on top of the outer. She undid the clip at the back of her head, and let her hair hang as she ironed.

On the roof in the darkness, she could feel him watching.

The children and I sat all around her, drinking water, not helping.

She looked at the children. "Baba's not here, is he?"

They didn't answer.

Her hair had grown. She must have fixed it herself, it was no longer uneven. It fell in wisps around her neck, like smoke.

She looked at me. "You don't mind, do you, Bea? It's hot in here."

Adel went back to his friends on the rooftop.

"I'm in love with a foreign girl," and he pointed to the maid with the children, and the American beside her in the window. They looked out to where he was pointing, through the dark to a bright yellow kitchen. They watched the blur of the running children. They watched Nisrine's back as she ironed.

"Adel's in love with a foreign girl," they teased, "he won't guard anyone but her," and they meant me, the American. They laughed and looked over at my bright hair through the window, because Nisrine was a maid with her back to them, they couldn't see her beauty. An American was foreign.

HE WROTE HER POEMS. He wrote them on tissue paper, one copy for her, one for him, and stuffed them in pink plastic bags we used for the bathroom, tied up the bags, and threw them onto the balcony where she would find them. When he learned she didn't read poetic Arabic, he memorized his poems to recite to her. He included long, annotated, simple Arabic translations, and when she didn't understand, he went through the poems line by line and explained them, so she would know what his love meant.

To a Flower, Even Prettier than Jasmine.

I love jasmine flowers, explained the simple
version. *Really, I love jasmine. And you're more
beautiful even than the jasmine.*

And She Will Know Inshahallah,
That after Her there are no Women.
And before her only Dust.

*You are the only woman for me. I will always protect
your honor, and I will always tell you the truth.
And I tell you, anything you want, I'm yours, it's
before you. I've talked to you for three days, and
I've known of you for two months. If I've lied to you
one word—this is in writing! Let me record it in
writing! If I've lied to you, tell me in front of
everyone, You're not a man! I don't have a reason
to lie to you.*

For in the Desert, She Is All Water
In Her Arms I Rest from Thirst.

*You are my everything. Doesn't a man in the desert
thirst just for water? And if he has water, doesn't that
sustain him? I'm an open book, Nisrine. Pick a year
and I'll tell you. I'll help you. Ninety-four. I was
nine. My first love. Pick another. Please, Nisrine,
pick another. It is beautiful when a woman questions
and a man answers. I tell you everything. I relax
when I tell you, I relax when you know.*

And like the White Flower Alone She Sits,
Shining in the night.

*Point to the jasmine, Nisrine. No, point to the
jasmine. Who's my life? Eh, who's my life? That's
right, Nisrine Kusnadi, she's my life.*

I have not talked about my own feelings, or Nisrine's, these
will come later. For now, I give you Adel, who could talk and talk
about love, and write poems and poems of jasmine.

His images were dust and desert and the full moon. There
were no trees in his poems, and no ocean, he rarely saw those
things, and he wrote from what he knew: a vast desert, a gray station. Here, white was a rare color and so he wrote and wrote about
jasmine, because the only white he'd found to describe Nisrine's
heart was the jasmine flower in bloom.

ADEL'S LOVE STORY

ADEL'S PARENTS WERE IN LOVE. He believed in romance. Now, he was in love with a dark-haired maid who had a husband and a child, and whose time was not her own. But he believed in equality, and simply loving. If he loved Nisrine, she would love him, too, and that would be enough for them, she would need no more than his affection. He'd keep loving her and she'd keep loving him, and through their love everything else, like jobs and children and education, would fall into place. He believed in his parents' love, and it gave him courage to believe in his own.

He told his mother about her.

"I'm in love with a foreign girl."

His mother said, "Foreign. Paris?"

"From the East."

"New York. Does she like our big city?"

It was not New York.

"She loves it. She never gets out."

His mother said, "That's your fault, donkey! You take her out. I'll give you money. Is she blond like you?"

"No, dark haired."

"Dark hair, light skin?"

"Face like the full moon."

His mother said, "I like those girls. She loves you?"

"I love her."

"If you love her, then she must love you."

Adel realized that, like his friends at the station, his mother did not understand what he meant by foreign. So he tried again the next evening. His aunt was over with her maid. They sat in the living room and sent Lilene to get tea in the kitchen.

"Kiss for your boy, Lilene," Adel teased. He turned to his mother. "Mama, why's the maid sulking?"

Adel's aunt said, "Do you know what Lilene said to me today? She said, I'm slow, Mama, because I didn't get a shower." She laughed. "She plays me like a child."

"Did you say that, Lilene?"

Lilene didn't answer.

His mother said, "Lilene's been eating wool."

"Are you eating wool, Lilene?"

"And after all my sister feeds her," Adel's mother said. "Adel's in love with a foreign girl."

"A foreign girl? What's she like?"

And he could have told them, but they were worried about Lilene.

THOUGH WE DIDN'T KNOW IT THEN, Baba met Adel twice in those months through his own dealings with the station. Any man who'd been in prison signed a contract when he got out to go to so-and-so station at so-and-so hour twice a month, to report on all he'd seen and done, and this contract lasted the rest of his life.

At the station, it was the young policemen who interviewed ex-prisoners, because it was a brainless job: they asked questions and recorded the answers, they didn't judge or think. Adel had interview duty three to four times a week. He sat at a tin desk in the station's basement. The men came in and took a number from the red number dispenser (the visa lines in the American embassy used the same number dispensers), and when Adel was ready he called the next number in line as if the men were waiting for a service, to refill their cell phone minutes or buy a blender, but instead they gave information.

When Adel did his interviews, he didn't judge; he simply asked appropriate questions and recorded the answers in a thin notebook with puppy dogs on the front.

Now, I have this notebook. It sits before me.

Rashid Halwani, Adel wrote, *height 1.83m, age 25.*
Work: Still no news. Suffers from unemployment.
Activities: Neighbors had to leave, grandmother died? Destination unknown. Back Sunday night. Saturday was Sheraton Club. Russian women danced with him, he didn't buy them drinks.

Money spent: 10,000 lire. Whose money: Father's.

People seen: Mahmood al-Ikhwan, Kerim Morsi, Simo Mustafa, Firas al-Kurdi.

If Baba came on the right day, Adel interviewed him, too:

Hassan al-Bakari, height 2.1m, age 66.

Work: Bookbinder, 25 orders filled last month.

Binding: Book for children learning to pray, <u>Positions of Prayer Made Easy</u>, new edition.

Adel didn't ask Baba about the women of the family. It was not polite, and these interviews were only cursory. He asked about business, who Baba had seen, and where he'd gone. They were interviews to record movement, to find out revolutionaries, to make sure that Baba loved his government. They were not to ask the health of the family maid.

Nevertheless, after Nisrine, Adel began to take a special interest.

By Baba's name, he wrote: *(Sir) Hassan al-Bakari. Height 2.1m.* He added little notes to himself, character judgments.

Work: Bookbinder (of the Quran the Karim).

Orders filled: 25 (smart man!).

Adel ran through his list of questions twice, and then looked up at Baba. He didn't want the interview to end.

"Maid?" he asked finally, when all other questions eluded him.

"I don't have a maid. My wife does."

"My mistake," Adel said.

There were officers above Adel who read his reports, and after Nisrine, they began to notice a change in Adel's writing. Adel had friends at the station, but even his friends, who believed in love, knew it was their duty to watch him, and as he fell more and more in love with Nisrine, they found Adel's back was turned to them more and more often. They went to the officers.

"Adel loves a foreign woman. He won't guard anyone but her."

Because Adel was his father's son, the officers went to his father.

"Adel writes soft reports. He notes character and intelligence."

Adel's father summoned him to the living room.

His father asked, "Why are you a policeman?"

"To serve my country and my religion."

"Why else are you a policeman?"

"To serve my family and my father; I am my father's son. I do not want my father's money, I want my own money. I must hold myself to the highest standard. I must carry myself so all will know I am my father's son."

His father asked, "Do you guard foreign women?"

"If they are in this country, I must guard them."

"And only them?"

"No, everyone."

"Especially them?"

"Especially citizens."

"That's not what I've heard," his father said. "You are the son of a man, now act like one."

Adel was indignant.

"I do," he said, "I do guard everyone! I guard the women and the children."

For a few days after that, Adel guarded ten minutes toward Nisrine, ten minutes with his back to her. But, he loved her. In his love, he soon forgot this caution. He met her again in the garden. He watched Dounia run around them in circles while he made up stories to show he didn't care about social standing.

"In our home," he told Nisrine, "everybody's equal. The maid is equal. The gardener is equal. Even my father's driver, who's Yazidi, is equal. You know what that is?"

"They worship fire."

"They worship the *devil*. But my father doesn't care. Except, we don't let him use the bathroom. You know what Yazidis do to wipe? They take their finger, and they rub it on the wall. You go into a Yazidi house, there're brown streaks all over the wall. But even in the bathroom, my father says, you have a choice: *ya* water, *ya* paper. No finger, that's for your own bathroom. Not mine, I'm Sunni. Understood? But the driver goes outside."

She laughed at his equality. "That's like saying a maid sleeps on the floor because she chooses to."

He didn't mind. Love was laughing, and telling.

"I dream of where you sleep, Nisrine. You tell me a story."

So, she began. "My mother is never jealous. To a fault, even. Sometimes, my father wants her to be jealous. He believes if she's jealous, it means she loves."

"You're not jealous of me," he told her.

"I am." She was not. She didn't have time to be jealous, her time was not her own.

"Once, my father put on his nicest suit that he only wears for weddings. He took the motorcycle and left without telling my mother where he was going. My mother fried rice in the kitchen. She read in the living room. We asked her, 'Mama, Baba left in his nicest suit, don't you want to know where he's going? Maybe he took some money.' My mother controls the money, but my father knows where to find it. My mother didn't say anything. She continued her frying. When it was dark, she got ready for bed.

"Finally, my father comes home three hours later. He's smelling of cologne he put on before he left. He asked my mother, 'Don't you wonder where I've been?' 'No, I trust you.'

"And because she trusted, he told her. He'd been over to his brothers', harmless. He beat them at cards, he handed my mother the money he won. You see, men think it is nice to be jealous, but my mother knew love is trusting."

And caring, and telling.

"I trust you, Nisrine. I love you for your soul in pink pajamas."

When she was on the balcony and he was far away, then he would raise one arm, and if she raised hers, it felt like the sky could connect them.

There were things he wanted: a stolen kiss, sweet words (he was the one between them who said sweet words), a peek, close-up, beneath her little white veil.

Nisrine was less sure in their love than he was. Sometimes she would be sweeping and, though she didn't mean to, she would forget him, drawn by the pull of her home. She worked against this; she would rather remember him, he was here before her, someone to make her happy; in the quiet dawn when he called to her, he thought he could hear her heart beating.

Adel understood why she forgot, and he waited patiently for her to remember.

He had always been a man who liked to be in the center of things. He liked the crowds of the city, big streets, and men in groups who took up the whole sidewalk.

But now, after Nisrine, Adel preferred the city from above; that was where real lives were lived, away from the spit and mucous of the gutters. He knew now that, like Nisrine, the real citizens of this city did not know the outside of four walls, except by a door's peephole, and this was a beautiful existence. He'd learned so much, loving her, about how faraway, up-above love worked, he knew he could go on forever if she would let him, he needed only a roof to stand on, a window to look through. She'd told a story about jealousy, but he trusted her, like she trusted him.

. . .

Then one day, she wanted to use his cell phone.

"What about Bea's phone?"

"It doesn't call internationally."

"Who're you going to call, anyway?"

"My husband and my child."

Pause. Love was trusting.

"I thought you said he was a drunk."

Adel felt his nose and eyes fill up with pollution. He took out a tissue, but the wind stole it, so he wiped his eyes with his leather jacket; it marked him as a policeman.

"Whatever you want, Nisrine. You want my soul? I'll give you my soul. You want my cell phone, I'll give you my cell phone. You want me to throw myself into the street?"

He made to jump down into the street where the cars were passing.

"Adel. Stop playing."

He stepped back.

"Ah, see? See, you'd miss me."

Adel left the roof that afternoon to buy a cell phone card for one thousand lire. Nisrine tried to give him money. She wanted to drop one hundred lire down to the garden for him.

He told her, "Forget it. I don't need your money." Phone cards cost one thousand. One hundred lire was nothing, it was like not giving him anything. She insisted, he was doing her a favor, she wanted to help. She got out the one hundred lire very carefully and wrapped it in the plastic bag he'd used to send his last poem. She had only two hundred lire total. She didn't go to stores here, she didn't know plain bread cost thirty.

Adel walked one block to the phone card kiosk, which was small and square like a cracker, and overwhelming. Here before him were all the colors that Nisrine might like: purple of the cookies in their cellophane; brown and gold of the American candy wrappers; puffed blue of the chip packages, all in row upon row of shiny color. He would have given her any of these. He'd spend his whole salary pampering her, if she'd let him.

But, she wanted his cell phone. He wondered how many units she would use up. He tried to make as many calls as possible on the way back, out of sight behind the station, before he hid the phone in the garden for her, so not as many units would be wasted. He knew this thinking was wrong, but he had just put on more units recently. It all seemed very expensive, to have to buy another phone card so soon.

Adel went home that night to dinner, and tried not to think about Nisrine. On the table were bulgur and cubed meat and tomatoes. He wanted his mother to pass the tomatoes. He opened his mouth to ask her—

"Mama, how much does it cost to call Indonesia?"

"Who's in Indonesia, Adel?"

. . .

After dinner, Adel helped his mother clear the dishes. He followed her into the living room.

"Mama," he asked, "what do you wish for me?"

"I wish you a good life and a good job and a loving woman," his mother told him.

"A foreign woman?"

"Fine, then. A foreign woman."

"What kind of foreign?"

"Any kind. London. Paris. Baghdad. The important thing is she's like us, see? Free, like the Europeans. We and the Europeans have a lot in common. We eat well. We read the same books. We can all speak English together. What would we do if we couldn't all speak the same language? For example, if she knew Chinese instead of Arabic. Then where would we be? We'd be mutes!"

"Mama, I'm in love with a foreign girl."

"You told me, New York."

"Not New York."

"It's OK, Adel, don't tell me the specifics, I don't need to know. Let those stay special for you."

ADEL FOUND HIS PHONE in the garden the next morning. He looked at the dialed numbers; Nisrine had dialed three times, at 6:04 a.m., 6:07 a.m., and 6:36 a.m. He looked at the received calls;

they hadn't called her back. He couldn't remember what button told him the units he had left.

He went up to the roof and found her on the balcony, hanging the laundry. She had a clothespin in her mouth, and Baba's wet pants in her hands dwarfed her. When she saw him, she held the pants with her chin, so they touched the ground, to wave at him. Her nails were painted red so he would notice them.

He shrugged and held up the cell phone.

"Everything OK?"

She nodded.

"That's good, then."

Adel could be so cheap sometimes. Here he was, hoping she wouldn't ask to call again, at least for a month or two—until she somehow got her hands on another hundred lire—and yet he loved her, and she loved him, and afterwards everything was beautiful between them.

Adel watched her working.

He watched her baby the children.

When Madame took a nap, he called the house phone. She brought it out to the balcony, to talk to him. Across the street, he pointed down at a clothing-store awning. "Anything you want from here, if there're clothes you like, I'll get them for you."

She looked out at it. "Thank you, but you don't have to."

"I love you. I want you to love me the way I love you."

"I love from the heart. I don't love for money or clothes."

"I know, I know. I just want you to know. Do you want more units on my phone?"

"No, thank you, it's OK."

"I'll get more for you."

"You don't need to."

"I want to. I know people. Next time you need to make a long-distance call, Nisrine, just ask me."

"Really, when I love I love from the heart." Sometimes, though, she needed things.

"I know. You're a very good girl."

They watched the cars streak past below them.

Adel asked, "Want to know what I told my mama and baba about you?"

"What?"

"I said there's a girl, foreign. But I don't see her as foreign. I see her, better even than the Arabs. She doesn't go out naked, you know, you dress long like the Arabs do; when I look at you, I don't see parts of your skin."

Nisrine laughed.

"*Aiwa!* Your laugh is my sun! Wink for me."

"No, I can't."

"Come on, just once. I want to see how your eyes close. Wink for me."

"Adel!" But she was smiling.

"That's right, one little one."

For Adel, things were all blond looks and clean sun. Here across from him was his woman. They were both prisoners to a small space—she the kitchen, he the roof of the station. In this city, life happened on the ground level, in the streets and markets and doorways. High above in their lonely jobs, they were both happy to have company. It made even mundane tasks, like patrolling and sweeping, exciting.

I saw Nisrine keep her back graceful and straight when she swept, because she knew Adel was watching. She woke early to smooth her pajamas and her scarf so when he looked in, he would see how beautiful she was, with her graceful arms and her straight back, and he would think how well she held herself, even sweeping. (Someday, he might see her alone, close-up: the possibility of this kept their hearts beating.)

Adel watched her as she cooked and cleaned and babied the children. He could not hear half of what she said, even when she spoke to him, because her accent was strong, and it was across a street, beside a garden. But, he understood her perfectly. He had a job on the roof, and Nisrine who never left him. Everything Adel wanted was here before him; he always knew where to find his woman.

GAS CANISTERS

OVER THE NEXT WEEK, I watched while Nisrine forgot her
Arabic. She no longer remembered the word for frying pan, she
called it "A Hot One." She remembered all the words for romance.
She called the teapot "Sweet Whistler." She called our glass cups
"Stars."

Madame shook her head. "It's like she's regressing. She has the
vocabulary of a teenager." She held up a white plate. "Nisrine—
hello, Nisrine! What's this?"

Nisrine couldn't remember. "Is it 'A Full Moon'?"

Of course, I was jealous. I was still the one who liked him first.

I asked, What about her husband?

I asked, Did she love him? Did she care I'd liked him first?

Nisrine met me with kindness. She made it up to me with careful
confessions.

She caught my eye across the table.

"I ask him, Why do you love me? Why me? There are a million women for you. And he says, Nisrine, because you cook and clean and I see you take care of the children so well. I tell him, Yes, I can cook and clean." When I first arrived, Nisrine had told me she dreamed of a big house and a restaurant. She was soft for men who liked her cooking.

We like to be loved for the things we appreciate about ourselves. I liked words and meaning. I wanted to be loved for my calm, collected scholarship and despite my messy hair. Madame would want to be loved for her soft skin and her shapely arms.

Nisrine rarely left the apartment. She and I had once shared deodorant like perfume, and when there was a joke, she was the one who poked me: Laugh, Bea. They're only joking; laugh, Bea.

Now, she pointed out the window and asked, Why do you love me? And her policeman said, Because you cook and clean and take care of the children so well, and these compliments made her happy.

Her policeman.

I asked, What about her duties?

I told Dounia, Don't change in front of the window, you don't know who is watching.

I asked again, What about her husband?

Nisrine's hand went to her heart. "I love him."

I ignored Nisrine all during lunch, when she burned the bread motioning to me.

Nisrine sent me a note. On the front was her English. On the back was Adel's poem.

> *Bea, you are my friend here, you can help me please*
> *I want to use your hand phone because I want to*
> *talk to him this is very important for me if you*
> *want to help me you can give me the phone just*
> *one minute, please.*

I loved Arabic for its flexibility. For the way it could be written on any surface—glass bowls, mosque tiles, grains of rice—and, unlike English, it didn't need a straight line to make meaning, or to look pretty. I knew all ninety-nine words for love in Arabic. I'd studied them, in case they came up in the astonishing text. I knew the words for lisp and mistake. I knew the word *khiyata*, which meant sew, and *khiyana*, lover's envy.

I wanted to be flexible like Arabic, generous on every surface. But I couldn't help comparing Nisrine's policeman's poems to the notes I received: a reminder from Madame that rent was coming due; a note from Lema to ask if I'd seen her wooden brush; the note from Nisrine, *Bea, you are my friend here, you can help me please.*

. . .

I wrote her back:

> *You're my friend, too. Do you love him? Do you*
> *care, I liked him first?*
> *The streets these days are crazy.*
> *I'll let you use my cell phone, but it's running out*
> *of battery.*

THE GAS CAME in round metal canisters, painted white. There was a man with a donkey and a wagon, and in the winter he covered the canisters with a wool blanket to keep them warm. In the summer, he covered them with the same blanket so the sun didn't get to them. On the street, he would yell through a megaphone so we knew he was coming. I heard it early in the mornings, *"Bismillah alrahman, alrahim,"* he said, as if, instead of selling gas, he was praying, and that was how Madame knew to get out all the used-up canisters, so she could send them down with Abudi for full ones.

At Madame's, the children and I didn't touch the stove. There was a safety valve you had to turn at the top of the canister, inside the cupboard, to let the gas out so you could cook. Madame showed me carefully when I first arrived. Meticulously, she turned it on and then off. I turned it on, and then off. But the children and I weren't allowed to touch the stove, only Madame or Baba or Nisrine.

Nisrine had Adel's poem. She stood by the stove, and I stood beside her, bent over it, quietly reading.

Abudi was a big boy. He poured tea into a glass by himself, without asking.

Abudi said, "Oh, the tea!"

Nisrine said, "Abudi, you naughty boy! You think your fingers're tough like mine? Water's all over now, you always make work for me."

Abudi ran. Nisrine grabbed him.

"When you need something, ask me."

"Mop it up, Indonese."

But Nisrine pointed out the window, at the police station.

"You see that man? He knows what you do. That man loves me. He knows if you're a bad boy with me, he's watching you."

Abudi wriggled.

Madame came in. She said, "Nisrine, you're scaring him."

Abudi was wriggling and wriggling. He kept wriggling until he wriggled all the way out of his shirt, and as he did, he knocked against Nisrine and me, and the poem flew out from between us onto the floor, and Abudi left us alone with Madame in the kitchen: his shirt, Nisrine, the poem, and me.

Madame came over and picked up the poem where it had landed. There was tea on one side of it; she wiped it off. From her angle, she couldn't see which of us had dropped it.

"Is this yours, Bea?"

"No—yes."

It was Nisrine's. I wasn't going to betray her.

"It's for my studies."

Madame raised an eyebrow. The poem was faceup. Across the front was written, *To My Flower, the Jasmine.*

"Are you writing love poetry for your studies, Bea?"

I glanced at Nisrine.

"To practice vocabulary."

"Oh! To practice vocabulary." Madame looked between us. She handed me the poem, and watched while I carefully put it in the binder I took to my lessons, between my grammar exercises.

Madame said, "You know, that's an old trick, to practice Arabic with love poetry, your tutor's not the first. Men are always saying about how there are ninety-nine names for love in Arabic. Don't believe them. Those names are love for God, Allah. There are ninety-nine names for Allah, and his name means love. That's different than romance."

While we were still in the kitchen, Lema came in. She was on the phone with her friend who loved a Christian boy. Her friend got in the car alone with him. She'd dyed her hair for him, which meant he'd seen her without a veil. When Lema got off the phone, she tried to decide if she should tell her friend's mother about the Christian.

I said to Lema, "I don't think you should. She trusted you, love is something secret."

Madame said, "This is a girl who needs to be stopped."

I said, "Maybe she'll learn on her own to stop loving him. It does no good to tell her mother."

Nisrine said, "Her mother will lock her in the house."

"No, she won't." Madame gave her a hard look. Then, she gave me a hard look. She turned to Lema. "Why don't you let me talk to her? Bring her over here and let me tell her what she's doing is wrong."

"No, you stay out of it," Lema told her mother, but Madame could not stay out of it, she had to be the center of everything.

In the evening, we all sat around the living room drinking tea, and Madame flirted with Baba. When he asked for sugar, she gave him her pinky.

"Bea's writing poetry in her class," Madame said, looking at Nisrine.

Baba raised an eyebrow. "You remember the story of Qais and Leila, Bea?"

Of course I remembered it.

Baba reminded me anyway. "Qais was exiled to the desert because he wrote his love poetry."

I said, "It's for class. To practice vocabulary."

Abudi quoted, "'To my flower, the jasmine.'"

Baba said, "Careful, Bea. Tutors are like ex-prisoners. They talk to the police."

Nisrine responded to Madame's suspicion with worry. Her brow furrowed. "Do you think Mama suspects?" she asked.

I was unsure.

"Do you think Mama won't want me anymore?"

I was still feeling jealous; even so, I couldn't imagine anyone not wanting Nisrine. But Nisrine shook her head, still worried. "I can't stay here if Mama doesn't want me. I have to make her want me."

"She wants you."

Just as I couldn't imagine not wanting Nisrine, I couldn't imagine Madame's without her. She was a part of this place to me, the way Baba's books and the sky were part of it: integral, close to my heart. A policeman didn't change that.

And Nisrine had so many reasons to stay: her family, whom she sent money to, her house, her contract.

Anyway, it had just been one poem.

Nisrine said, "My father works for other people. In my family, we all work for other people. But it is a point of honor with us, we only work where we are wanted. We are good, we are always wanted. I have to try harder."

"She wants you." But it was true that Madame had begun to watch us.

I felt a deep affection for Nisrine, who was so good, and had so much honor. I decided to try harder, too, like her.

BUT WE WERE NOT DONE with worries.

The winds blew up from the north and over our small mountain, and brought Baba home, worried: new friends had been taken. He couldn't meet anymore with other men in dark parlors, there weren't enough of them left.

"I think there's a rat," Baba said. He meant an informant.

I knew about informants; they were the reason we didn't talk in taxis, or to bus drivers, because the bus drivers and taxi drivers often talked to the police.

Madame had once told me a story about how her mother had almost gone to jail because of an informant. Her mother studied to clean this country's first airplanes, but she fell in love with a man who hung on her every word, and so repeated everything she said to his policeman friends. It turned out, some of her words were dangerous.

"What happened?" I asked.

"They took her for questioning, and when her lover realized what he'd done, he was so upset, he wanted to die, he hadn't meant to inform on her. In the end, my mother was released. She never talked to him again."

I thought about this story, and how here, talking could get you in trouble. Baba and his friends were secretly writing their free elections document, but they could not write it and finish it if one of them was a rat, or the government would find out before they were done. I imagined them publishing that document; if you could go to jail for talking, then what might writing about elections do?

Whenever I thought about these things, I felt a small tug at my heart for Baba, who did what he wanted despite the danger.

Like Madame and Lema, I was both proud and fearful for him: proud that he was creating a brave document; fearful of what that might mean for him, and us. Just as I could not imagine life without Nisrine, I could not imagine this house without Baba.

And yet, in his own way Baba was also an informant; an ex-prisoner, he had his interviews with the police.

"Yes," Baba said when I asked about this, "but everyone knows this about me. They know when my interviews are and what I'll say. I'm not the dangerous kind. What's dangerous is not knowing."

"Not knowing?"

"Sometimes, people can be rats without wanting to be, because they slip up at the wrong time, or they're friends with the wrong person."

Like the man who informed on Madame's mother because he was blinded by love, an accident.

"This is the most terrible part of our country, Bea," Baba said. "That it is possible to be a good, brave person, and still also a rat without knowing it."

AFTER THAT, Nisrine and I tried very hard with Madame. Neither of us wanted to be rats. She sang to Dounia and braided her hair every morning, while I made the beds.

There was an attic above the kitchen that you needed a ladder to get to. Nisrine didn't like small spaces, and she didn't like ladders, but she followed Madame up to sort the jars in it. They squatted inside, backs hunched, and separated the olive oil from the jam. (Nisrine muttered, "I will not have an attic in my house.")

I stood at the bottom of the ladder, and sometimes they handed me down a jar. Nisrine's hands shook when she did this, because of the small space. Sometimes, though, from up above, I heard laughter. They talked about boyfriends. "Who was your first?"

"I was thirteen, the neighbor."

Nisrine said, "My husband is a rooster. He likes too many women. When he liked me, he left a rooster in my yard to crow his love. All day, I sat inside with my mother and listened. I thought it was very romantic. I should have known, once a rooster, always a rooster."

Madame said, "The first time Hassan saw me, he said, 'You are like wine.' He had come to give me sad news. I was good, I didn't drink wine, I'd never tasted it. I thought, God is Great and against drink, but now I have to taste it, Hassan said I was like it. After a while, I decided I could love Hassan like he loved wine."

After the attic, Nisrine cleaned inside all the other cupboards. She took a ladder and a cloth to dust the ceilings. Still, Madame walked in to find the freezer door open and Nisrine's face pressed against the window.

"What are you looking at?"

"Toward the river."

"The river's the opposite direction."

MADAME WASN'T THE ONLY ONE who suspected foreign women of having lovers.

At the end of the week, my student ID expired, so I went to the library to get a new one. At the security window before the entrance, a young policeman attended me.

"Name."

I gave him my name.

"Address?"

I gave him my address.

He looked up.

"Across from the police station!" he said about my address.

"Yes."

He looked me over. "They say the policemen there like foreign girls. Where did you say you were from, again?"

"America."

He shook his head in admiration. "America!"

I said, "I think you're mistaken. The policemen don't like me, they like a different foreign woman."

But, this policeman couldn't be convinced. He stamped my papers and told me to come back for my new ID in two weeks.

"Two weeks? Can't you make it sooner?"

He smiled, shook his head again. "America," he said, "you have policemen lovers. If you want a fast card, ask them."

I tried to stamp out the blond one from my heart. I was always on the lookout for him; when I saw him, I turned my back.

I loved Nisrine for her singing; for her determination, and her jokes. We were working together, to try harder so Madame would be happy and not suspect, but I still envied Nisrine her shoulder blades, like two birds kissing while she folded the laundry.

Nisrine tried to include me.

She guided my arm back and forth before the window.

"Wave, Bea. He'll wave back."

When I first met Adel, I was told he was a real Qais, which meant a deep romantic. I had first liked him for this image, even before I knew him; before I read his perfect poems and understood how he loved words and meaning, just like me.

If Adel was Qais, then that made Nisrine Leila. I had once dreamed of being Leila. I looked over at her now: her straight back, the long curve of her neck. Nisrine made a beautiful Leila. She didn't seem to notice. Her beauty was a part of her like any; like her smile or her thoughts, not the only one. I loved this about her, too, and I wanted to think like her, I didn't want it to matter. Her hand on my arm, making me wave, I thought, I could stay right here forever.

But, at the same time, I wondered, if he was Qais and she was Leila, then who was I?

Wave, Bea, he'll wave back, and he did.

Because she had told him to.

While I waited for my ID, I went through the roles in my head. Leila's father: was suspicious of their love. Leila's new husband: was her punishment. I couldn't think of a role for me.

. . .

I tried again at the National Library. This time I went, determined to flirt my way to the astonishing text, like Nisrine.

At the library, there was a man and a woman behind the desk. I went up to the man. He was wearing the long beard and white robes of a religious scholar. I didn't care. I arched my back.

"Can I have a text?" I flirted.

The man looked up. He glanced at me once, then, with his eyes on the floor, he went to his female colleague. She came over. "Can I help you with something?"

"I wanted a text."

She told me I could wait in the cage for it.

I said, "That man was helping me, he was going to get it." She looked over at her colleague, who sat in the corner, his eyes trained studiously on a blue computer screen.

"That man is religious and a faithful husband. Here, we don't flirt with faithful men."

At my next Arabic lesson, Imad had a new workout machine and his idea was for Maria and me to run on the machine while we were reciting Arabic. To make it more natural, he said. To make it so we didn't think before we spoke. The verb for using a machine in Arabic is *laub*, which means to play, so after that, in our lessons Maria and I said things like: I want to play on this machine now, and the sweat was coming off of us; I want to play on this machine, are you done playing on the weights, Maria? I wanted to play on the bike. The sweat was coming off of me.

Imad said, "Say something in Arabic, Bea. The first thing that comes into your head. Say it with voweling."

But all I could think was, I wish some policeman would write poems for me.

On the phone with my mother, I complained: Nisrine couldn't stop talking about a policeman, as if we didn't have enough to worry about with Madame's suspicions, and Baba's revolution, and my studies.

I asked again and again, What about her husband? Until Nisrine turned around: "Stop, Bea."

But then one morning, I felt a hand on my shoulder as I was sleeping.

"Bea, I don't know what to do, I love Adel, but I love my child in Indonesia."

I tiptoed through the silent house, Nisrine giddy as sunlight before me. We passed the living room, and did not wake Baba, who was asleep calmly. We passed through the kitchen; Nisrine took my hand and pulled me out, onto the balcony.

"We had trouble in Indonesia, just like here. Before my child was born, we had storms, and on the other side of our country, a tsunami. I was very pregnant with my child. The winds came and beat our little house; outside, you could hear motorcycles banging. My husband had hung wind chimes all around our house. We had taken in the flowerpots and bicycle, but no one had thought to take the wind chimes in; they blew around, and they chimed so loudly we couldn't sleep. All night through the storm they clanged, but no one wanted to go out in the rain to take them down.

"In the middle of the night, we woke with a start. There was a crash. A tree had fallen over half our house. My husband opened the door of our bedroom, and rain and torn-up leaves came in. But, where were we to go? We closed the door again, and got under our bed, so if another tree fell, the frame might protect us, and listened to the wind. It howled outside our door; the rest of the night we stayed like that, and my child felt my worry. He was awake in my belly the whole night, his little legs moving.

"In the morning, there was water and a wasteland. From our house where the tree fell, we could see all the way to the ocean.

"I walked out with my child in my belly. My husband went to see about staying with his family, and to get food. When he came back, I was still walking. The landscape was so different, I didn't recognize him in it. He tried to kiss me, and I lowered my head as if I'd just met him, so he kissed the top of my head. He said, 'There is so much ocean here, even your head tastes salty.' After that, we went to live with my husband's family. I took care of his mother and aunts, the old women, and they all touched my belly, they said, 'This child survived a storm, he is already lucky.' Let him be good, I prayed, and he was, from the moment he was born, he was.

But my husband couldn't find work, he didn't rebuild our house, he wasted our money."

In the morning light, a lone wagon moved along the sidewalk, behind the garden, out of sight.

"I love Adel, Bea, but I miss my husband. He gave me a child."

Nisrine was a maid with a growing heart. She had left a family that she loved, and now she worked to build a new home, to replace the one that had been broken; to send her family money, to start a new life. And yet, to be happy in her work, she had to find other loves; this was her dilemma—how to love here, and love there; to work for one love, she needed the excitement of the other.

We leaned out over the railing, arms crossed, feeling the air on our faces, feeling policemen in the air.

Then, from the edge of the rooftop, we saw a hand waving.

"It's him!" Nisrine cried.

The hand stayed there for a moment, waiting. Then, slowly, as Nisrine uncrossed both arms to wave back, Adel appeared. His hair was golden. There were brass medals on his chest.

She used my cell phone to call him.

"You talk to him, Bea."

"I don't know what to say."

"You talk to him. He knows I very love you, Bea. I very very love you, you know."

I said, "Hello?"

"Hello, Bea! Does your father have a car? My father has that one, in green."

There was a red car driving below us.

Nisrine took the phone.

"Hi, *habibi*, you love me?"

I could hear him on the other end. "It is beautiful when a woman questions."

She kissed my cell phone at the mouthpiece. "Bye-bye, go on now, bye-bye, this is Bea's phone. Say good-bye to her, you love me, bye-bye."

"Your face glows like a star. I'm an open book. Ask me anything."

"Bye-bye, this is Bea's phone, you love me—"

"—bye, Bea!"

"Bye-bye!"

She hung up.

I took the phone.

On the roof he raised one arm to the sky.

Inside, we heard Madame waking. We ran to the kitchen. From the window, we could see him waving.

Arabic is a phonetic language; in this way it's economical. Each word only gets the letters it most needs. My name had two sounds, the *b* and the *e,* and so in Arabic I got two letters, not three, and in colloquial speech my name wasn't a name, but a preposition: "Bea" can mean on or around or in.

Nisrine was also a foreigner, but her name was more common than mine, and it had three sounds, so she still got at least three letters like the Arabs did, whether she wrote her name in Arabic, English, or Indonesian. In Arabic, you could write Nisrine's name two ways, because there were two letters that made the sound "*sri*." With a soft *s*, these letters were also the root for commerce and purchase. With a deep *s*, Nisrine's letters formed the root for virtue, and to overcome.

Some days, I felt like my name, a lowly connector. I felt our names were the difference between Nisrine and me: She was a noun and a verb in Arabic. Her name acted and moved and had money, while mine just got stuck in between.

But there is a lightness to love, even when it's not your own. There is camaraderie in waving. She took my hand. Adel stood on one side, we stood on the other, waving and waving.

Nisrine had once told me about a word that meant maid, and heroine, and moveable house. It was not from her language, it was from her mother's, who came from a different island. But in Nisrine's town, the concept was the same.

"When I was young, when a family wanted to move, the town all got together, picked up the house from its old spot, and set it down in its new one. That was what we called moving. We took our houses with us."

Nisrine's last house had been moveable. It had been built by her brothers, and migrated to her husband's family after she was married. A moveable house was like a maid's, or a heroine's, heart. It had to be flexible, but strong; to make a place for itself anywhere, no matter the surroundings; for those who counted on it, to always be a home.

"Did you like living in it?"

"Of course, Bea. It was my house." The one she had lost when a tree fell, before the birth of her child.

She smiled. "Moveable houses are beautiful, but they are hard, and old-fashioned. A storm comes, you have to get twenty people to sit in it, so it doesn't fall over. There wasn't glass in our windows, only wood shutters; at night, the bugs blew in. When I go home, I'm going to build a cement house, with cement foundations. That way, my child will know permanence."

Permanence: cement that doesn't give when a village lifts it.

I had grown up in a cement-foundation house that didn't move; I'd lived in that same house, on those same cement foundations my whole life, and the truth was, I found myself trying to get away from them. I had come here to feel different, because at home, I hadn't felt enough.

Still, I was glad to know Nisrine's house's story. It gave familiar words, new definitions.

A moveable house was one that went with you, that a community came together and lifted.

Community—that which doesn't just force you to stay, but helps you to move forward.

Home—what you take when you go.

I looked at Nisrine, thankful to her for giving me these new meanings to think about.

Foreigners in this city, Nisrine and I each had our dreams; she her house, I my text. I was glad to know about Nisrine's dreams; I was glad not to dream alone.

· · ·

Out on the rooftop, Adel was still waving. Nisrine sighed, smiled, waved back.

"He's from Allah, Bea. He knew I was all alone here, I had no one." Though, she had me beside her, my arm in her arm, waving. "My god, Allah, sent him down to me."

THAT EVENING, I read over the story of Qais and Leila, searching for good characters.

Nisrine saw me. "What are you doing, Bea?"

It was a silly thing. "Nothing, studying."

But, she watched my finger, how it stopped over certain people—Leila's mother, her sisters.

Nisrine asked, "Have you heard of the shepherd?"

I had heard of the shepherd. He met Qais after he was exiled to the desert, and helped him find water.

"He did more than that," Nisrine said. "He cared for Qais and became his friend. Some say he's the one who kept Qais's poems, and later made them famous."

"Really?"

"Yes, you should look into it."

A keeper of poems. It wasn't like being Leila. Still.

"Maybe I will."

UNREST

IN THE NIGHT, there were gunshots. In Madame's apartment, we all jumped. Baba rushed to the window to look, but he couldn't see anything. He ran out and opened the door, which led to a hall without windows. The neighbors were also at their doors. We all stood at our doors in the apartment hallway, talking about the gunshots, and whether this meant there were antigovernment protests. There were rumors of a takeover.

Madame herded us all onto the sofa in the living room and boiled water for tea. On the radio there wasn't talk of the gunshots. There was a special on the life and times of a famous poet.

Baba said, "I'm going to look around."

"Outside?" Madame asked. "Stay with us, Hassan. It's dark outside. You can't even see."

But Baba was already looking for his glasses. He searched the sofa. He searched a pile of fresh-bound books.

Madame sighed. "We are such cowards," she said. "Everyone heard gunshots, and no one even went to the balcony to look. We just stand around in the hall, where we can't see anything and the police can't get to us. Except Hassan. Hassan's the only donkey stupid enough to move himself tonight. The neighbors are all asking one another and no one knows what happened because no one will poke their head outside to see."

After the gunshots, there were more pro-government rallies. They followed early in the morning. But this time, fewer people came. We weren't allowed to talk about politics in front of Dounia: schoolchildren were talking, and their parents were being arrested. You could tell which side the parents were on by the children's games of tag: one side was the president's, the other was democracy.

At my next lesson with Imad, Maria and I both showed up early, because there were pro-government rallies scheduled for the afternoon, and the buses would all be diverted. We didn't want to end up on a bus accidentally bound for the rallies.

At our lesson, Maria was sulky and didn't want to play on the workout machines. She watched Imad and me pedal the bicycle and do sit-ups.

"I miss Starbucks," she said. "Don't you miss Starbucks, Bea? I miss donuts. And United Colors of Benetton. I want to go into an air-conditioned mall, and know they'll have a United Colors of Benetton."

Imad said, "With voweling, Maria. Repeat that with voweling."

But today, Maria wasn't interested in voweling. Today, she was interested in the gas sanctions and night gunshots, how it all made her tired of being here.

She kept having to blow her nose, so Imad kept stopping the machine to hand her tissues, and when he did, his arm passed right next to my ear.

After a little while, Maria decided she couldn't study today, she was too distracted, so she got her purse to leave before the rallies began.

On the workout machine, I was struggling like Maria. I couldn't help it. I kept thinking about gunshots, and Nisrine, who I was trying hard with, and American drip coffee.

When Imad returned from walking Maria out, he held a tissue for me.

"Your eyes are puffy," he said.

"Really? That's so strange! It must be allergies."

I went to the mirror to look at my eyes. Imad followed me. In the mirror, I could see his whole apartment. It was all straight lines and empty space because he lived alone. Not like Madame's. At Madame's, there were sofa covers and floral prints and on the walls were the round curves of embroidery.

Imad asked, "Is everything OK, Bea?"

"Of course."

I was here to study. There were gunshots in the street, Baba might sign a free elections document, I couldn't access the astonishing text, and I was here to study.

Out the window, we could hear the beginnings of a rally. Imad went over and fiddled with the radio to drown out the sound, but the radio stations all played folk songs for the rally. I was used to this.

When he couldn't find any good stations, Imad turned the radio off. "I'll sing to you instead," he said. "Do you know Assala, Bea?"

I didn't.

"Do you know Warda?" Imad asked.

Everyone knew Warda. So Imad sang me a song by Warda.

"*I ask you, what would I do if you left me?*" he sang. "*You say, love another. But I can only love another if he looks like you. I can only love two men if there are two of you.*"

His voice was low and soft the way a forest is low and soft and far away from this city, which made me love his voice, the way I loved faraway things right then: the calm of land and space out a back window. Madame's apartment only looked out the front.

When Imad was done, he went to his window. "I hope it rains soon," he said. "Do you like the rain, Bea? Here, we love rain. Rain is like blue eyes, we think it's special."

I said, "My mother used to sing to me."

Imad said, "Consider me your mother."

After a moment, he said, "You want to know what I sing to my mother? *She will be with me all my life, my woman . . .*"

It was a nationalist song. The woman was the country. It sounded like a national anthem. When it was done, he sang a song about a man who was imprisoned in the Golan, so the man made his body a blank canvas on which to write his love. A text of love. It reminded me of the astonishing text, which had the power to move even scholars and old men. I still felt I must read that text. I kept trying, and the days in which I didn't read it kept passing, and as I studied more and more, it had begun to take on a sort of background urgency, a small ache at the back of my heart, where Nisrine and Adel also were.

Imad asked, "Do you have any jokes, Bea? To make the time pass, until the rallies are done."

I had jokes. But they were ones I'd heard Baba tell his friends against the government. I didn't think I could repeat those, even to Imad.

So I told him one in English, instead. "What did the girl olive say to the boy olive?"

He didn't know.

"Olive you."

Imad liked that one.

He said, "A man has never slept with a woman before, and his friends tell him, 'Come on, let's go find some girls.' So they find a nice cat—that's slang for girl, Bea—and they leave him alone with her. And she asks him, 'Is there anything I can do for you?' and he says, 'I'd like a cup of coffee.' She makes him the coffee. She says, 'Is there anything else I can do for you?' He says, 'I'd like some dinner.' She makes him some dinner. She says, 'Is there anything else I can do for you?' He says, 'No, I don't think so.' She says, 'All right, then.' He says, 'What are you?' She says, 'I'm a cat.' He says, 'And I'm an ass.'"

Imad laughed very hard at his own joke. He asked me for another one. While I was thinking, he sang me another Warda song.

"*I love you* leila *and* nahari *(night and day)*." *Leila* means night in Arabic.

I thought about this fact, and about the suggestive joke Imad had told. Qais and Leila never kissed, they didn't have the opportunity, they only loved from afar. As I thought of this, I realized Nisrine and Adel had probably never kissed. They blew kisses, imagined kisses—did they miss the real ones?

This whole time, I had been dreaming of a love like theirs.

Outside, the rally was passing. Behind it came a man leading his goats, and the man and the goats were herded off to the side by policemen. The land swelled up around them, rocky and ugly and cement ridden.

Imad said, "Where have you gone, Bea? To America and back?"

"No, I was listening."

So he sang me another song. And as Imad sang, the rally disappeared down the street, and again we could see the empty city, sprawling up the hillside, and it was also ugly, and Imad's voice filled the room, and I realized he had sung me all the way until the rally was done, and I could go home. He had a beautiful voice.

At the door, Imad kissed me on both cheeks, like the French did, even though neither of us was French.

"I'm glad you came today."

I said, "What else would I do?"

"I just want you to know how glad I am."

IMAD HAD SUNG ME A SONG in which the prisoner who is far away writes his love onto his bare chest. He has neither pen nor paper to move her, only his imagination, his memory, his arms. And so, he makes himself the text.

That night, Adel taught Nisrine to write Arabic. Because he was far away, he enlisted my help.

"*Ayn*," he called over from the rooftop, and on the balcony I drew the letter *ayn*, a long half-oval shape, with a curved little tip on the end.

"So this is you?" Nisrine asked him. "This is your letter?"

"Adel" started with *ayn*.

"Yes," he told her.

She traced the letter, learning it, letting her finger linger along its oval part, rub up against the tip.

She made an unexpected joke. "Are you curved like that? A woman likes a curve like that."

I thought of kisses, and Qais and Leila.

Behind us, the sun was setting. Before us, Adel's face grew red as the setting sun.

Sometimes, I still felt him like arak.

Nisrine and I laughed.

Nisrine was still trying, and I was still helping her try.

When we came in from the balcony, Madame was in the kitchen. We hadn't noticed her.

Madame said, "The tea boiled. You were nowhere."

"I was sweeping."

Madame didn't say anything.

Nisrine took the pot, dumped out the boiled leaves, and began to make new tea. She hummed a song in English.

Madame said, "That's a love song. I know it from the radio."

All the radio's songs were love songs. Madame didn't see it that way.

Sometimes, my trying with Nisrine got in the way of Madame and me. At breakfast, Baba reached out and touched my cheek.

"Bea, you have a zit."

Madame said, "Bea eats too much chocolate. That's why she has zits."

Here, I rarely ate chocolate. But, we were no longer talking about zits.

Madame said, "She should know better, shouldn't you, Bea?"

For a while, Nisrine tried to keep her distance from Adel. She turned her back, the way he once had when he worried about his father.

I found myself trying both with Nisrine and with Madame; trying to both help Nisrine, and keep my own distance.

And yet:

She came out to the balcony early in the morning, and she was right on time, but he was already on the roof, waiting. He smiled when he saw her. They both stood on their opposite corners, toes dangling.

I looked up from my studies, and saw them draw their love out of the air. The length of Nisrine's arms when she called to him. The curve of her neck, which was just like the curve in my book of the Arabic letter *ya*.

Adel opened his arms, showed her his eyes. Though I have not talked of it, these were beautiful days for him, too; his poems tell me this. After Nisrine made the joke about the shape of his letter, *ayn*, it stayed lodged in his stomach.

Theirs had always been a faraway love; she had taught him the beauty of two eyes, ready, waiting to be given.

He watched her veil, the way it swept down over her forehead, caressed beneath her chin. What if I were that veil? he thought. What if I lived there, in the folds beside her cheek, where I could always reach her neck, always kiss her skin?

Nisrine came to him, sometimes serious, sometimes joking.

"Run away with me?" she called, and he knew it was a form of playing. He closed his eyes to imagine running: the thud on cement, the light sway of her breasts, her hand on his arm like silk.

There was another consideration for Adel; this was his father. He still had not told his parents about Nisrine—it sat, a light silence, like her husband, between them. They both had reasons they couldn't run. Still, they played at the image.

"Anytime you want, darling."

"And the money?"

"We'll get an oil contract. Do you know any American oil companies, Nisrine? I have a cousin."

On the roof, he would do anything for her. He gave her his chest, his mouth, by touching them.

"You want my soul?" He touched his throat. "Anything you want is yours." As if to take it out, he made a cutting motion.

He thought of his father: *You are the son of a man.*

"When you are sad, Nisrine, go down to the river. Look out and think, I was loved by a *man*."

And Nisrine?

I woke often, now, to her light touch on my shoulder. And we would tiptoe again and again out to the balcony, the dawn sky before us, my cell phone in her pocket. Mist lay over the city like lace.

Nisrine had her own worries. She had a child and husband to love. She had to grow her heart to want to stay, and now she worried, too, about if Madame still wanted her. She couldn't lose this place, it supported her. She couldn't lose this place, it would be against her honor: *We only work where we are wanted.* She still had to save money, to build her house.

Because Nisrine and I were equally foreign in Arabic, I didn't notice her accent or her mistakes when she spoke, especially if it had to do with love, or cooking: in both these subjects, she had a vast vocabulary.

In English, though, I was the better speaker, and so unlike Arabic, in English I noticed when Nisrine put words in the wrong order, or when, instead of using an adjective for emphasis, she'd just repeat.

"I love Adel, but I very love my husband and child in Indonesia."

For this reason, because I was attuned to it, I heard the light shift in her speech, when it finally came. No longer, "I love him, *but*." Rather, *and*.

"I love Adel, and I love my child and husband." An inclusion. "I love them, I pray for them, and they love me."

I READ UP ON THE SHEPHERD.

The story goes that in the desert, Qais made friends with the other wanderers. He met a lonely shepherd who took pity on him and helped him find water. Qais recited his poems to the shepherd, and they became friends. And for the rest of his days, this is how Qais lived; in love with Leila, beside the shepherd, so in some ways (though, not in the same ways as Nisrine's and Adel's and my way), it became a love story of three: the yearning lover, the missed beloved, and the shepherd, who listened over and over to Qais calling, *Leila!* while he minded his sheep.

Before my next Arabic lesson, Madame told the children to dress, and we all went to the shop down the street to pierce my ears. Madame chose two tiny blue studs like eyes for me, to match my beady ones. The children were all dressed up, like this was an event. They stood around, watching, while the man took my earlobe in one hand and a gun in the other to shoot the studs in. When he was done, he rubbed in olive oil. Madame nodded in satisfaction.

"See, Bea, now you're a woman."

Lema said, "Bea's tutor won't recognize her, she's wearing earrings."

I was still used to thinking of Adel that way, not Imad.

But I said, "Yes, he will."

But Madame agreed with Lema. "No, before you were a book, you don't wear makeup. People can't love books, Bea. They love women."

On the way back, we saw Nisrine on the balcony. She was reaching up to the sky, as if she could touch it.

Madame said, "What's she doing up there?"

Now, she drew a heart in the air with her hand.

"Maybe she's hanging laundry."

"There's no laundry basket."

SMELLS

IN THE AFTERNOON, I sat in the living room, reading and eating chocolates that Dounia kept serving me. We were playing a game. She had on a shirt and a hat that covered her eyes, and she was talking to me as if I were a crowded room, and she were the waiter. She wrote down the name of everyone who wanted a piece of chocolate, as if I were everyone and each one of me wanted chocolate, while I tried to study.

There was a smell of gas, so I opened the windows but it still stank.

Madame came out of the bedroom, where she had been applying face cream and listening to the news about the rallies. "It's that one," she said, meaning Nisrine. "She left the gas on."

Without our noticing, the smell of gas had crept over the apartment, and now it was everywhere. It seeped up from the soft carpet and heavy curtains.

Madame went into the kitchen, where Nisrine was working, and the smell of gas was wafting.

She said to Nisrine, "You're trying to kill us. Am I paying you to kill us?"

Dounia stopped her game, and she and I sat very still with the chocolates and my books in the living room, listening. We tried not to breathe. We tried not to die from the gas, or from angry Madame. There was shouting and banging. Madame came back to the living room, and the smell of gas in the kitchen was so strong, she was almost gagging.

"She has no mind, Bea. No mind!" Madame said.

Dounia and I sat still as the books and chocolate. I was sure it was an accident. Nisrine had been trying very hard with Madame. I was sure it could all be fixed, she had not left the gas on on purpose. I picked up my book, but the gas was too strong. I set it down again.

I said to Madame, "I'm sure it was an accident."

Madame wasn't listening. "You see why I don't leave the house? She could have killed us."

"Is Nisrine OK?"

Madame said, "I don't care if she's OK, she could have killed my children."

For a moment, Madame and Dounia and I sat thinking of all the people she could have killed.

It was Nisrine.

I said again, "I'm sure it was an accident."

Nisrine came into the living room. She blamed it on Abudi, but Abudi hadn't been near the stove. She'd turned the gas on for the tea. Then, she went out to hang the laundry. When she came back, the flame was off but the gas was still going. She said she was sorry.

"No good, no good," she said about herself, and Abudi. "I'll do better, Mama, I promise."

But, Madame wasn't listening. "This one is twenty-three, Bea, twenty-three," she said, as if Nisrine was not there. "She should know better."

Nisrine didn't say anything. Her eyes were red and squinting from the gas.

"And those eyes, *those eyes*. I don't like her, she looks at you screwy, God, those eyes!"

Nisrine got a very still look on her face. She hesitated for a moment, then walked back toward the kitchen.

Madame said, "I don't like her anymore. I want a different one."

I got up to follow Nisrine, but Madame grabbed my hand. "Stay here with me, Bea."

She sent Dounia to go check on Nisrine, and see if she was doing the mopping. "Go see where she is, Dounia. I can't bear to look at her."

The gas crept over our apartment and got into all the furniture. It seeped into the afghans. It clung to the embroidered wall hanging: *God Save This Home*. It seeped from the moist bathroom. It lingered in the closets and the fresh pillowcases: *She could have killed us*.

It was Nisrine. It was an accident, it could have happened to anyone.

Nisrine drew hearts in the air on the balcony, Madame had seen her.

She could have killed us, the gas seemed to say.

When Baba came home from work, Nisrine had packed her bag. The children and I were still up, so Madame herded all of us out the door, into the car where Baba was waiting. Nisrine sat on one end beside me and Dounia didn't sit on her lap, Dounia sat on Lema's lap. There was a traffic jam.

"Are you OK?" I asked.

Nisrine didn't say anything. She hadn't said anything all day, since Madame said she wanted a new one. I had tried to think of things to make it better. I had said, We don't want a new one. Neither Nisrine nor Madame was listening.

We sat very still in the car, until Abudi remembered he had an appointment with the dentist to tighten his braces today, and we had forgotten to take him. There was a flurry while everyone tried to decide who to blame.

"Now you remember? *Now* you remember?"

"What kind of mother are you, anyway?"

"Abudi Kareem, you have a cell phone. Program your cell phone."

Nisrine sat quietly, with a determined face. The traffic moved very little. When we were close, Baba double-parked and he and Madame got out.

Madame said, "Don't worry about the rest of your things,

Nisrine. I'll bring them to you tomorrow. Just take your pajamas to sleep in."

Nisrine didn't move.

"Where's she going?" I asked.

Madame said, "Hurry, Nisrine."

"Nisrine, where are you going?"

Baba opened the back door so Nisrine could get out. He reached down to take her bag in one hand and carefully closed the door behind her with the other.

Nisrine said, "You are like my father." He was facing the children and me through the car window.

"You stay here," he told us. "Bea, watch them." He made sure the doors were locked from the outside.

Nisrine said, "I love your children like my children."

Dounia and Lema and Abudi and I watched out the back window as they left. None of us knew where Nisrine was going. None of us knew if she would be back. One minute, we had been eating chocolates in our living room. The next, we were here; it all seemed very sudden.

We watched her small back bob between Madame and Baba. Normally, Nisrine was very strong, she lifted large pots of boiled meat by herself, but her suitcase looked heavy for her. Halfway to the building, Baba stopped and tried to take it, but she wouldn't let him.

In the car, Lema's hair kept coming undone beneath her veil.

Lema said, "Dounia, help me do my hair." You could see the ends of her ponytail sticking out.

Still looking out the car window, Dounia stuck Lema's ponytail down the back of her shirt.

"Not like *that*," Lema said. She pushed Dounia's hand away. "Stupid."

Lema took off her coat and threw it over her head, to fix her veil in secret. Dounia tapped the coat. "Is it fixed yet, Lema?"

"Leave me alone!"

Dounia and Abudi both pounded on the coat.

"Is it fixed yet, Lema!"

"Ooh, you're so stupid!"

In my head, I made trades. All the vocabulary words I knew, for Nisrine to come back. What did vocabulary matter? It could be learned again. There was no one like Nisrine.

Lema came out from under the coat. Her veil didn't look any different, except there was no hair coming out the bottom now.

Nisrine used to fix Lema's veil. She once sewed a miniature white one for Dounia's Barbie.

I thought how hard she had been trying. I thought of Adel. I tried not to think of Adel. I thought of us linking arms, waving.

She'll be back, I thought, to reassure myself.

Abudi said, "Let's open the door and close it again."

I said, "Leave it alone, Abudi."

She'll be back, she'll be back.

Abudi climbed into the front seat. We looked for Madame and

Baba. The cars were going around us, because Baba had double-parked, and he was taking up a driving lane.

Eventually, she did come back. She still had her black bag, and she walked between Madame and Baba. Baba was smiling. Madame wasn't.

At the car, Nisrine opened the door herself, and got in between us. This time, Dounia sat on her lap. Madame said, "They don't have any other maids right now. We have to keep this one."

In the backseat, relief came off of us like sand.

I had wanted Nisrine, we had wanted her. Now, she was back, we hadn't believed she would really go away.

We rode home, pinching her arms to make sure she was there, and hugging her. Nisrine was quiet. When we touched her, though, we felt her warm skin like silk, and she patted us back.

By the time we got home, the children and I had begun to pretend that this had never happened, and Nisrine had never almost left. We brushed our teeth, and Dounia hung off Nisrine's waist.

In the kitchen, Nisrine set her bag carefully on the floor; we brought her warm milk, and again we hugged her; we were all hugging and laughing, when Madame came in. "What's so funny?"

Nisrine turned around. She said, "I'm sorry, Mama. It won't happen again. I'll do better."

Madame went up to Nisrine, and sniffed her beneath her neck, at her collarbone. "You stink, haha. You stink, that's funny."

Nisrine grew very still in the center of us.

Baba asked Madame, "Where are you going?"

"To check on the washing."

"Come back afterwards and sit with me," but she wouldn't. All that evening, Madame wouldn't sit down in a room where Nisrine was, she complained Nisrine stank.

The night passed. We were all happy Nisrine was back, except Madame. For Madame, she could not get rid of the gas. It was all she smelled when Nisrine entered a room, and it lingered and thickened, until finally in their fights, we began to forget how happy we were, we forgot how we would have missed her if she had gone and, like Madame, all anyone could smell anymore was gas.

The next day passed. We had aired the house and Madame told Nisrine about using the stove again, but the smell lingered on and on.

LEILA

THE NIGHT BEFORE THE GAS, Adel dreamed of Nisrine. She was wearing a red sari—in the dream she said, "We're Muslim, we don't wear saris!"—but that was how it went: red cloth, a green mango, her child against her chest. He could see how the cloth hung off her shoulder, and he imagined the small white lines that marked the rapid growth of her breasts after her baby, her dark nipple like soil.

Later, Nisrine would wonder to me about the things he said: the mangoes, the stretch marks. How did he know about stretch marks? Was this his way of showing her he really was worldly, he knew about women? She was struck by how even in his dreams, he imagined imperfections. Like old men she knew in her country, who left imperfect lines along their hand-blown glass, not to attract the devil. Like the Arabic phrase *mashallah*, which wards off the evil eye from beauty, a superstition. In his dreams, he dared not dream too much; he gave her stretch marks, bitten lips, a bad ear, a blue toenail, as if these small troubles might charm away any larger ones. As if, with delicate white scars like lace on Nisrine's breasts, then he and she would both be free to love whom they wanted, when and where they wanted, for the rest of their lives, and their love could reach perfection.

Police are human, they like security, and they like when they feel it often. For months, Adel had watched Nisrine every day; he had waited for her in the morning, his toes at the very edge of the roof. She was a maid, her routines were not her own, and so very soon in their love, he had come to predict her—to know at six, she would be in the bedrooms; at seven, she would check the gas on the stove. Predicting was a way he loved her; he knew all her angles through the window, the shadows her arms made when the sun hit them; and he claimed this knowledge, the way other men might claim a woman by the taste of her skin.

When the gas happened, Adel was on duty. He watched the family gather in the kitchen. He saw us behind a glass window, a horrifying picture. Nisrine faced Madame, her back to him. He knew she must be worrying. He waited to see if we would hit her, if we did he knew he'd feel it as if we'd hit him. He wondered if he should call a policeman. This is the power of love, it made him forget, *he* was a policeman.

Do you guard foreign women? his father had once asked.

I guard everyone.

So Adel watched, and did nothing.

. . .

He was alarmed by his inaction. He loved Nisrine, deeply. He sat down on the roof to think, put his head in his hands, then stood up ready to help, but his father's words came back to him: *Do you guard foreign women?* Adel was a lover, a real Qais, a policeman, his father's son.

To his great embarrassment and horror, he watched Nisrine leave that night, and still he did nothing.

She was gone two hours. Adel didn't go home to dinner with his mother, he waited on the roof to see what would happen. He watched our darkened windows, and as he watched, he felt the cement of the roof and the sky slowly close in on him, until there was no room for breathing. His heart swelled and swelled, until it was so full it stopped, because there was no room for beating. So he did his work without a heart, and without breathing, until finally at the end of the night Nisrine returned, and he saw her again with her little bag through the kitchen window.

She came out to him with her arms open. In his heart, he jumped into them.

"Nisrine, where did you go? I thought I'd lost you. My heart's breaking!"

She laughed it off, shrugged. It had been her mistake, she didn't want to talk about it. "Run away with me?"

"Anytime you want, darling."

An old joke between them.

He knew something was wrong, or she wouldn't have gone. Because Nisrine left our apartment so rarely, it made two hours seem like a very long time.

She must have known he was upset, he was gray as the station.

Adel looked out and saw for the first time how vulnerable the woman he loved was. How small—her stomach barely came up to the railing, she was barely taller than the children. When she leaned against it, her elbows stuck out like ungrown wings.

And then, from deep inside him he felt another feeling— growing, spreading through his legs and chest.

He wanted to touch her.

Theirs had always been a faraway love. She'd taught him the power of a look, of two eyes ready, waiting to be given.

He *needed* to touch her.

She had once made a dirty joke about the shape of the *ayn*, his letter. That joke had stayed lodged in him for days. He wanted her to make another. He opened his mouth to ask her—

"Nisrine, can I put it in?"

"What?" She was still distracted by the evening.

He felt the heat rise to his cheeks. But, she hadn't said no.

"I said—can I put it in?"

In the old stories, like Qais and Leila, there is a faraway kind of intimacy. These lovers rarely touched. But they made love with their eyes, and poetry, which was the same way Adel's father said angels made love in the Quran. It was the way the Archangel

Gabriel made love to the Virgin Mary, from afar, and gave her a child.

Nisrine said, "I thought you were a virgin."

He was. "I am if you want me to be, Nisrine, can I put it in?"

Nisrine moved to the edge of the balcony. She had been distracted, but now she leaned out the way she had when they first loved. When, to give her his eyes, all he had to do was touch them and she would understand.

"Run away with me, Adel, and we'll really love."

"Can I put it in?"

"You love me, Adel?"

He wanted her here, now, even this way, imperfectly. That was how much he loved her.

In the Quran, even virgin love begets children.

"Can I put it in?"

"You can put it in."

"Nisrine, I love you so much, I can feel your soft soul all around me, it's like being covered in the most beautiful flower."

Afterwards, he leaned against the wall of the roof, and she leaned on the railing, sweaty and heated.

The worry had come back to her face, so he complimented her to distract her.

"There's a donkey here who thinks you're so pretty, he could write a poem."

"Is there?"

"Yes. Do you know him?"

"Yes."

"What do you think of him?"

"He's a donkey." But she said it sweetly, and they laughed and laughed.

He opened his arms to her. "I love you so much, honey, don't ever leave me, my heart's breaking."

They had once played a game where she was in trouble, and they thought up all the ways he could save her.

"Flying!"

"With a fire hose!"

"With wings!"

Now, she said about his broken heart, "Don't say that!"

"But it's true."

Silence. She said, "Bea thinks we're like Qais and Leila."

Leila had left, and Qais had done nothing.

He held out his hand.

"See me shaking? That's not weakness, Nisrine. I shake because I love."

THAT NIGHT, I helped Nisrine put Dounia to bed, and our rituals seemed very sweet because we had almost lost them. Nisrine took Dounia's hands, I took her feet to swing her, in fun.

We peeked through the curtains into crocheted shadows of streetlights.

Nisrine said, "Bea, I have a problem."

I knew this. I could tell by the way she held herself, and Madame held herself, that in our house, there was a problem. I had felt this problem coming for some time, but I was still trying not to have the knowledge. I tried to live in the sweet moment.

"I don't know how to stay here. Mama no longer wants me."

"It will get better."

She had a contract and a child, and her father's honor: *We only work where we are wanted*. In a strange country, what are we without our honor?

"You've been trying, you just have to try harder."

But, I could see a faraway look in her eyes.

Nisrine said, "Do you think if I went to a new house, I could still see you and Dounia and Adel?" I did not think so, I did not like the idea of a new house.

Of course, Nisrine didn't think so either. She sighed, looked at me worried that she might leave, and for a moment, we felt all the differences between us. I had grown up in a world in which, when things got bad enough, you *could* leave, you had that choice; in which I expected challenges, not hardship.

Nisrine had seen each member of her family live a full life, yet still work jobs they would not have chosen, like she worked in a job she would not have chosen. I had chosen to be here. For a moment, this fact alone threatened to overwhelm us.

Then, she smiled. "Don't worry, Bea. I can't leave unless they let me."

Which was not completely true, but it relieved me. She said, "But my honor."

. . .

Once, a long time ago, Nisrine had taken my hand and put it over hers, to feel her heart. Now, I took Nisrine's hand and put it over mine, over my chest. She knew what I was doing. She felt for its beat.

"My, Bea, it's a strong one! Who's your lover?" Joking.

But, I had no lover. I was a young woman, alone, with love all around me; with Nisrine, and Baba's family for company. They did this. They had grown this.

"Try, Nisrine. Try a little more. We'll try together." Her hand on my heart. "This is where you are," I said.

TROUBLE

Over the next week, we at Madame's, and Adel through the window, all watched while Nisrine forgot her Arabic. Before, she had been distracted by love, and so called the frying pan "A Hot One." Now, she was distracted by her situation, by the trouble of trying hard in a home where she wasn't wanted. She simply forgot the word for frying pan, she called it nothing. She couldn't remember the word for cold. Nisrine, whose policeman loved her for her cooking, got sloppy with the dishes. She leaned against the sink and let the water soak her waist.

She forgot things, not only language. Madame found the milk boiled, and Nisrine nowhere. She left her hair bands in the bathroom. She left the freezer door open and last summer's strawberries spoiled.

Madame said, "I taught her cooking, cleaning, everything she knows is from me. And for this I pay her. *Haram*," and she forbade Nisrine from going out.

Nisrine had rarely been out.

Madame took all the dripping strawberries out of the freezer and dumped them in the wastebasket. "People come here from all over the world to study because here we have religion right. Not like in Indonesia. But I'm very nice, I can't beat her."

Madame forbade Nisrine from speaking English, and from touching the children, but then Dounia's hair was always undone, so she asked Nisrine to braid it.

Nisrine repacked her just-unpacked bag, and stood before Baba. "Return me. I don't stay where I'm not wanted."

In part, she was bluffing. She needed us still, she needed this job.

Baba looked at her. "We want you, Nisrine. I want you." And we did, we did! We needed her like she needed us. We followed her around, picking up her lost hair bands.

Nisrine had once told a story about a woman who loved the rainbow, so she turned into a bird and flew away. She started looking more and more out the window, as if she were seeing a rainbow. I whispered, Try, Nisrine, try. Because, I wanted her. It repeated itself like a song inside me.

She watched the V's of the mosque's doves.

But we had other things, too, to worry about.

There were rallies every Friday now, and in response, sandbag blockades went up all across the city. They sat plump and secure like fat ladies and the police hid their weapons behind them.

We heard about an international investigation, and secret protests. There was a new list of things from the government we could not do:

Speak on our cell phones on Fridays; we might be inciting unrest.

Gather in groups at night; it might lead to a protest.

Forward any political e-mails; the government was watching, our friends would block us.

Go down to any protests; these were for young men, they were using live ammunition.

In this city, there were two sides now, with the president or against the president, and you must choose which side you were on.

Of course, Baba was against the president. He had written a secret free elections document. We felt more and more how police watched him.

One day, Baba came home to announce the document was done. Now, all that remained was for each man to sign.

At Madame's, we panicked. We had thought the men would take longer to create it; we had thought we'd have more time to convince Baba not to.

Madame said, "You haven't signed it yet, have you, Hassan?"

He hadn't. He wouldn't, he mustn't.

Baba said, "Amal, we can't live in fear. We must work for better."

"What about your children?"

"Amal."

"What about them?"

Baba was torn. He knew Madame had a point. Outside, politics were becoming more and more dangerous.

Over and over, we heard the same late-night discussions.

"Don't, Hassan."

"I would have already, but I worry for you."

I agreed with Madame. I admired Baba for his bravery, but between jail and not signing, I would rather not signing. So would the rest of the family; Baba was the only one for whom this presented any dilemma.

We waited while he carefully weighed politics against family; bravery, against his love for us.

THE DEATH NOTICES were long sheets of paper, posted quickly after a death, but then rarely taken down, so they filled the city's walls right at eye level. One was even posted on the corner stop sign. It was spring now, almost summer, but it had been there since December. It hung across the red sign's paint, smoothed flat with glue. The air bubble in the middle obstructed the age of the deceased but not his name, not the large print announcing, as the cars slowed down, that he was Brother and Son, and now he was gone.

On our building, a new notice went up.

It was the death of our neighbor. He was on the side of the president.

His daughter, who was Lema's age, ran out into the hall, screaming. She tore her veil from her head, there in the hall, crying, and Lema went out to comfort her and began crying, too, in sympathy, even though they'd never gotten along.

After his death, our neighbor's family made food for everyone in the building. The guests poured in to be served coffee and sweets. Madame, who even before the unrest never liked the neighbors, accepted flaky pastries at the door from the same daughter who was crying in the hall, and lent them her teaspoons.

The daughter stood waiting while we hunted for them.

"Is this all?"

"Those are all the clean ones."

"I can wash them."

"Well, we need a couple ourselves to eat from."

All afternoon, from our neighbors' apartment we heard chanting. It started as a low, hollow sound and slowly grew—There is no god but God, Muhammad is the prophet of God—until our hall ran with it, and it shook the embroidery and the religious sayings in their frames.

"Oof," Madame said, "death, must everyone know about it?"

We waited until evening, and when the spoons still had not been returned, Madame sent me over to get them. I waited patiently at the door for them, and when I brought them home, Madame counted them carefully and we washed them again, even though they'd come back clean.

IN MADAME'S APARTMENT, there were also two sides now, either Madame's side or Nisrine's side, and if you talked to Nisrine, then you were not on Madame's side, and you could not be part of the family. Dounia tried to bake cookies with Nisrine in the evening. She was wearing Nisrine's apron, and they were both laughing.

Abudi came in and said, "Nisrine can't do anything right."

Dounia and Nisrine ignored him.

So Abudi hit Dounia.

"Stupid Indonese."

Nisrine kept trying. She took a cloth to the inside of the oven.

To assuage her honor, she thought up other plans to make money.

"Bea, do you know an American oil company?"

"No."

"Maybe you could find yourself one. It's good business. Adel has a cousin. He said if we find him an oil company to sell, he'll give us two percent."

I didn't like these plans, which involved her leaving. "I'm a student, I don't know anyone in the oil business."

"Maybe I could talk him into giving us three percent. On one million, that's thirty thousand."

"But I don't know any oil companies."

．．．

So, she tried again with something else. "Do you have a big bag?"

She knew I had a big bag.

"I have too many clothes." She had had to leave some behind, during the gas scare. "I need a big bag, for when I leave, to put them in."

I was frustrated with Nisrine. I wanted her to try with Madame, not big bags.

Still. When Madame went to the bathroom, we got out my big bag from the closet and wheeled it quietly into the children's bedroom, where Nisrine slept, for when a miracle happened and she could leave.

WHAT SAVED NISRINE was the house she would build. Through it, she still loved this one, and her love made me see it differently: the beauty of our green tiles, like cold oceans; the width of our windows—from them, lying at any angle, you could always see the sky.

I imagined this must be how Baba had seen his house, with eyes full of wonder, when he first got out of jail.

Nisrine went from room to room as if she had been gone longer than two hours, touching our walls as if she were remembering them, long white roads that might lead her someday to her own home, that she took a bucket and a rag to each month.

She borrowed Adel's cell phone to call her family. I watched her from the kitchen, her shoulder hunched up to her ear to hold the phone. While she talked, she swept one-handed.

"What did they say?" I asked afterwards.

"They want me to be happy. They need money."

After that, for a time she didn't talk any more about leaving.

AND YET, there were still days of beauty. Madame got out her wedding video to show us. All of us had seen it. First, there was a still picture of Madame, fifteen years ago. She wore a pink dress. Its skirt flowed off the screen, over Baba's lap. Baba sat very straight and still in the video. Even fifteen years ago, he looked awkwardly tall next to Madame's flowing skirt and perfume.

"Which is prettier?" Madame asked us. "Me now, or me then?"

"Who is that girl in the picture?" I teased. "I don't even recognize her."

"I look different with makeup on, no? Which is prettier, now or then?"

"Both."

"No, choose one."

"Now, without makeup."

Madame nodded. "Hassan thinks so, too."

The film cut to the party. The couple was given a single glass of juice and two straws to drink from. The music blared, even through the TV screen.

Madame said, "Don't ask me what kind of juice it was, I don't remember a thing about it."

She looked over at Baba, who read by the window.

"Do you remember what kind of juice it was, Hassan?"

"No."

We fast-forwarded to the dancing. On the video, some women had dragged Baba to the dance floor. They made a circle around the new couple. Madame was dancing. She didn't look at the camera, she looked at Baba, dancing. There was glitter in her hair and it sparkled in the light on the video, as she slid toward him and away. She shook her chest at him.

And this is how, in real life, we also started dancing. First Madame got up. Like the video, she swayed her hips. She swayed over to Baba, and shook her chest. "Come on, Bea," so Lema and I both got up. Lema followed Madame's lead. She isolated her ribs.

I also tried to follow Madame. She danced over. "Hips, not feet, Bea. These are your hips." Dounia bounced around us like a teacup.

From his chair, Baba clapped loudly.

I asked, "What's the matter, Baba, you don't like to dance?"

Madame answered for him, "He's shy, can't you tell?"

Nisrine came in from the kitchen.

"What was your wedding like, Nisrine?"

"I wore a red dress. It was my sister's before me. I almost fell over, because the embroidery was so heavy."

We stayed dancing and dancing. And then, all of a sudden Dounia got tired of dancing, she began to knock into us instead, and the room came together, and as she knocked, we lost our balance, and we all fell on top of one another, laughing, our limbs still moving on the soft carpet like upturned insects. For a moment, I couldn't tell which of us was which. My arms were beside Dounia's head, which ran into Lema's shoulder, which lay across Nisrine's back. We had once been a fourteen-armed creature called Baba.

Madame switched off the TV. She said, "Look how happy Nisrine is, her husband's far away."

Nisrine said, "I'm not happy."

"Yes you are, you're all breathless and glowing. You see, Bea? Foreigners like it here. They don't really want to leave."

But, Nisrine was becoming more and more distracted. We saw it in the apartment, the way dust clung to the ceilings, hung from spiderwebs that gathered like chandeliers.

I noticed the dust in my books.

Before, I had scoured these books for ways to understand love. Now, I began to scour them for ways to understand Nisrine, for the right thing to say to keep her happy with us.

. . .

Nisrine was not trying, I thought. She just had to try harder.

At least she has love, I thought, and deep down, I still felt my own small wish.

Nisrine said, "If Baba leaves, I don't think I'll be able to stay in this house." She meant, if Baba was taken. Baba was the one who still wanted her here, Madame didn't.

At night, we leaned out over the balcony.

"What do you think about Baba?"

"I don't know. I don't know what to think."

"Maybe we could ask Adel to help."

But, Adel had not helped Nisrine when she left.

She sighed, puffed out her cheeks. "I want someone to *do* something for me, and I want to *do* something. We are always inside, and nothing ever changes. Why can't Adel sweep in and take me by the waist and kiss me, if he really loves me? Why can't he save me? Why can't we save Baba?"

We wanted to, so much.

Nisrine was always the first I turned to in our house, the first I talked to. Now, though, she no longer remembered all her words. Sometimes, you didn't know if she understood because no matter what, she nodded blankly. It made me lonely.

Nisrine had once told me about the word that meant maid, and heroine, and moveable house, and we had let our imaginations soar around it.

I began to see how the maid really is the house. How she makes the house—without her, we drifted, stooping at the corners to avoid the spiderwebs. And outside, unrest.

In April, the winds swept up the desert in the evenings, and the city had no hill to block them, only a small mountain. They pooled around the mountain, catching the air currents in hot, breathless spurts, they waited and gathered strength. In the evening there were small dark smudges of smoke like birds on the horizon. We kept the windows closed against the soot and the smell. Sometimes, Nisrine remembered to sweep the dust, but she might as well not have, because the winds blew through the house and left it dirty.

There was a cockroach in the bathroom. It had been sitting there all morning. Madame didn't kill it. She came into the kitchen and said, "Nisrine, we must mop the house today, it is just too dirty. There are bugs starting to live here, you hear me? We must mop the floors."

It was a small kitchen, and in the spring heat, it was beginning to smell of olive oil and macaroni. Nisrine was singing like she always did, and washing the juice glasses. There was a special sponge Madame reserved just for the juice glasses, so they didn't begin to smell like grease. Nisrine used the sponge to suds all the glasses. Then she used another sponge to suds our dirty spoons. While she washed, she hummed and looked out the window.

An hour later, the cockroach was still in the bathroom, beneath the sink. I thought about spraying water on it, but perhaps it could swim. I didn't mind, I left it alone. I went into the kitchen, where Nisrine was singing a love song. The glasses shone on the counter, very neatly. She was arranging the pots and pans. "*No one wants to see us together,*" she sang.

The cockroach stayed all day, until it was eaten by a rat in the evening. There was a scream from Baba in the bathroom. The children and I came running.

"Amal," Baba called. He turned to us. "Go get your mother. Tell her to mop the floors."

ADEL WATCHED ALL THIS, and thought how Nisrine was like a dove: hard to hold, hard to keep. She came out to the balcony, and sometimes it was as if she didn't know him. After their first love, there was not any more.

He said, "Nisrine, I think about you in that terrible house and I cry, and I cry." You love someone, and then they are in trouble and want to leave, and you don't know how to help them.

Nisrine had never seen her policeman cry. She had seen him laugh and play, the shadows of his face in passion.

He came to her to tell her he cried now, often. In Adel's Arabic, the word for crying sounded almost like the word for reciting a verse of the Quran: *aya, aya.* Adel's accent was thick like his mother's, and when he forgot to speak with education it was very thick, and the *q*'s came out *g*'s and *k*'s came out *tsh*, and he repeated the word for crying twice every time he said it.

"I love you, Nisrine, do you believe me? I *aya, aya.*"

But, Nisrine was losing her Arabic. She might have believed him, but she was tired. "Don't speak to me in your language, I don't understand you."

Adel had no other language. He might have touched her, but the sky lay always between them. They needed a new language, one that did not rely on words; they did not know where to find this.

"I *aya, aya,* Nisrine. I go to the rooftop, and I *aya, aya* alone."

It is hard to know what changes a person.

Adel had watched Nisrine grow tired; he had watched her veil slip. She had always been neat, her nails always painted red to entice him. Now, they began to flake. He still carried the feel of her soul around in him.

He had tried many things to help her over the past weeks: talked to her, tried to love her, given her his cell phone. None of it seemed to matter. Adel couldn't think what else to do. When Qais lost Leila, had he felt this? Was it what drove him crazy?

He went home to his parents, and didn't eat dinner. His mother noticed the change, how her son looked gray as the station. She went to her husband. "Talk to Adel. Tell him about loving."

So that night, Adel's father came to him.

"What's the matter?" his father asked.

"Nothing." Everything.

"You don't guard the way you used to."

"Baba, have you ever seen someone in trouble who you love, and you found when it came time, you couldn't do anything?"

The father looked at his son, in love with a woman he would not approve of. Adel's father had reared and groomed him to be a good guard, not to bend the rules, to know right from wrong.

"Adel, you're a policeman. You can always do something."

FCUK

IN THE MORNING BEFORE MY LESSON, Imad called: there had been more gunshots, and there was talk of more sanctions. Maria got scared by the sanctions, and she left for home on an airplane.

On the phone, I was surprised. Flights were something I planned for, asked my mother for, bought ahead.

"You can leave like that? One day, and you book a flight?"

On the other end, Imad's voice was urgent.

"Are you still coming, Bea? My students are my life. You have to come. Maria's gone, you're all I have left."

My lesson this week was on a classic love poem, by Ibn 'Arabi. I sat alone with Imad in his echoey apartment and read the poem with all the voweling. The poet talked about love that left him with a green heart. He called his heart a garden among the flames.

In the middle of the lesson, Imad got a phone call.

On the phone, he said, "Where would you like to meet? The Old City?"

I was sure it was a new student. The Old City was where all the foreigners lived.

Imad said into the phone, "I am not in the Old City right now." He was speaking very clearly, like he did for his students. "I will meet you at six thirty Friday, then."

He hung up.

"That was the government's Security Services."

I looked at him. "What do they want?"

"I don't know, they want to talk."

"I thought you talked to them every other week."

"I guess this is a special talk."

We began class again.

We moved to discussing the poem's imagery. We discussed the image of a green heart, and the image of the poet's love's hennaed eyes, which stood for marriage.

Imad said, "I'm sorry, but that call is bothering me."

I asked, "Should we stop?"

But he told me to continue with the hennaed part.

Imad said, "I'm not political, Bea. I'm a teacher."

"I know."

"Foreigners always leave. When it got hard for Maria, she went home. But who's left? Imad. He's been to London. He knows foreign girls, but he's from here."

We turned back to the poem.

Imad said, "I'm just worried about this Security thing. I have a business to look out for. I can't have problems with Security."

I thought of Baba. "I know you can't."

We read another verse. I was having trouble with it. Imad said, "*Ma'an*. Together. With *ayn*. That's a first-year word, Bea."

I said, "Sorry," but I was still having trouble with it.

Imad threw himself down on his workout machine.

"All I want is a British girl with FCUK underwear, and a small bit of product in her hair, who is clean, and has smooth legs, and I want us to lie around for a long time in our underwear, I don't want to take off her underwear for a long, long time. Is that too much to ask?"

Silence.

Imad looked at me. "I'm sorry, Bea. I didn't mean it."

I went over and sat down by Imad on the weight machine. He laid his head on my lap. He had warm breath and a soft mouth, like a garden. There was a little bit of product in his hair.

Imad reached up and pulled my curl. "Arabic hair," he said. "Did I ever tell you, your hair looks like Arabic?"

"It does?"

"Like Leila's hair in the astonishing text. It always surprised me, in that text Leila hardly has a role, she leaves after the first page, but you feel her everywhere because of the way the words are written. They curl just like her hair."

"Leila had curly hair?"

"That's how I imagine her."

I had always thought of Leila's hair as straight, like Nisrine's. I reached up to touch my own hair. I felt around my ears, to see if it was frizzing.

"Imad, what's the astonishing text like?"

"Beautiful. Astonishing, like they say, I can't describe it. Don't worry, you'll see it."

It didn't seem like I'd ever see it. I wanted to, so much.

"Did you cry when you saw it?"

"Bea, I had just come back from London. I was on leave, my father was sick, and I had to decide whether to stay with my father, or go back to London to finish my studies before my visa ran out."

"So, you did cry."

"I cried. In the text, after Leila leaves, Qais wanders around until he finds a shepherd who cares for him. It taught me about love, I guess. Not just romantic love, but other kinds. Family love. That one form of love is dreaming about someone, and another is staying with them."

I looked down at Imad's slick hair, his fine eyes and nose, like a sand hill. In London, did his nose fit in? I thought about Security and all Imad had given up in London, to stay here with his family and students, with me.

"Imad, if you were going to be a person in 'Qais and Leila,' who would you be?"

"I don't know, I guess the shepherd."

"Really?" Imad had just mentioned him, but still, it surprised me. That was the character Nisrine had given me what seemed a long time ago now, when I was looking. I liked the shepherd, he was a good man, but I still secretly wanted to be like Leila; I assumed Imad would want to be like Qais.

Imad shook his head. "Qais went crazy for love, and then he lost her. But the shepherd, he knew about friendship. He cared for Qais in the wilderness, and some say he's the one who kept Qais's poems. He stayed with Qais his whole life."

"He did?"

Imad nodded.

A keeper of poems. Someone who knew about friendship. I put this aside to think about later.

Imad asked, "Did you get your ears pierced, Bea?"

"Yes."

He fingered my earlobe, lightly. "I like it. Blue looks good on you."

I didn't have FCUK underwear like Imad liked. I only wore white Hanes that Madame said looked like a grannie's, and Nisrine was always complaining she must bleach. I didn't have nice under-wear, and I wasn't graceful the way I imagined Leila was, or Nisrine was, even when she cleaned. But here in this room, on this weight machine, I was all Imad had. And, he was all I had, too, so we kissed.

I opened my eyes. Imad was looking at me, his hand in my hair. Then, because it was soft and warm, we closed our eyes and did it again, and again.

So this was how it felt to be a lover, Leila.

Imad brushed his hand over my neck, along my collarbone, under my chin. "I like you with earrings," he said.

I said, "So does Madame," which made him laugh.

Imad walked me home. He made me promise I'd come again on Friday, even though I didn't have a lesson, so we could go to the

National Library together before his interview with Security, to finally see the astonishing text.

"Really?"

"If they let us in," Imad joked, "maybe I can kiss you in their cage."

I took the stairs up to Madame's instead of the elevator, to try and savor my light, giddy feeling. On my lips were Imad's kisses. On my lap, his moist hair product. In my head, the astonishing text.

When I got in, there was a message that my mother had called. News of the sanctions and gunshots had traveled all the way to her, and made her worry.

"I keep hearing about unrest," she said when she called back. "Is everything OK?"

"Well," I told her, "Maria left."

"Who's Maria?"

"The other student from my lessons. It's just me in class now." When I said this, I couldn't help smiling. I still tasted Imad's kisses. But, my mother took it differently.

She said, "You know, Bea, there's a family reunion in May. You could leave, too."

"I'll still be here in May."

"Yes, I know, but it's a big reunion. Maybe you'd like to come home for it."

"Come home early?"

You're all I have left, Imad told me. *We'll see the astonishing text.*

"For the reunion. You can always go back afterwards. Think it over, OK, Bea?"

That evening, the family teased me. They joked again about Imad's English name, Matt, and how it meant dead in Arabic.

"How is he, *Allah yerhamo*, Bea? Still Matt, God rest him?"

"I saw *Allah yerhamo* walked you home today, Bea. He's quite a Qais!"

I said, "My mother has a family reunion in May. She thinks maybe I should come home for it."

And it was Nisrine whose face grew very still, who said, "You mean leave?"

Nisrine had been wanting to leave. She didn't have a mother who allowed her. I felt my embarrassment.

"For the reunion."

Madame said, "You're not supposed to leave until September."

This reminded me of other news. I told Madame, "I have class again this Friday."

"Friday?" Madame said. "Friday's a family day. I thought class was Tuesday and Saturday."

Nisrine was looking soft and still, her face to the window.

Lema shook her head. "What about your tutor, Bea? Matt *mat, Allah yerhamo.* Where else will you find a dead boyfriend, if you leave?"

IMAD WAS NOT A REAL QAIS, despite what Lema joked. He didn't even want to be. He was steady and kind to me, and I'd liked the warm weight of his kisses.

I followed Nisrine to the bedroom. "Imad kissed me."

"He did?"

Normally, this would be a small celebration between us.

She was thinking of other things. "Do you think you'd really leave, Bea? You're happy here."

I was. I was happy, and she was part of it. I still hoped Nisrine would be happy, too, that things would get better, and we could find a way.

Nisrine said, "Maybe when you leave, you'll take me with you."

"Haha, that would be nice!"

We lay on the bed, and built homes out loud, from our imaginations. In my home, Imad put all his best books. In Nisrine's home there was good food, and family, and Adel's jasmine flowers.

Then she said, "I don't care anymore about houses."

"You don't?"

She sometimes teased by saying things she didn't mean. I thought she was teasing.

"I don't think I'll ever build my house."

"Of course you will."

But, she shook her head. "It's a feeling I have."

I wasn't sure what to say.

"It's just a house, anyway. Why do I care for a pile of cement?"

Why do we care for anything? It is our nature, I wanted to tell her, what we do as humans. I knew that I for one loved strange things, like words and books, but I had never questioned that love, or wanting to love. Why not want? I had never questioned how much I cared for Nisrine.

And, Nisrine had never before questioned how much she cared for Dounia, or Adel, or rebuilding her house. It was a dream for her future, for her child's comfort, the reason for countless mornings, face pressed against the window, a cream-colored rag in her hand, searching for spots. She was beginning to dislike even the future.

I stared at her until she sighed and gave in. "OK, Bea. I'll build my house. Sometimes, I think everything would be all right, if someone would just be on my side for once."

Nisrine had been asking and asking, and Baba had done nothing, and Adel had done nothing, and I had said, *Try, Nisrine,* as if telling her to try might help her.

And looking back now, I want to step in, stand up, say, I am with you, I'm on your side, let's walk out right now, I'll find a new family for you, or if not a family, then something else, certainly we can avoid what is destined to happen next, certainly together, we can do something—we don't need to wait for Adel, or Mama or Baba, why did we always wait for them?

But, we lived in a small world, where everything we did was watched, by Madame or police or the neighbors. The feeling of being caught is something real: cramped legs, like a cramped mind—over the next weeks, this feeling would increase, we would feel more and more trapped, until finally, we found ourselves so utterly locked in, there was no way out. For this, we paid a very high price.

But, that comes later. Now, in this room, I still believed that love was staying, that as long as Nisrine was here, everything would be OK, that our tragedy would be her leaving.

We returned to talking about kisses. Nisrine wanted to know what Imad's felt like: breathlessness, a deep conversation.

"Bea, what do you wish for me?"

"For you?" I tried to think of all we both wanted. "I don't know, your new house and your son and great lovers."

"Thank you."

"You're welcome." Pause. "What do you wish for me?"

She thought for a moment. "Freedom, to be who you want in the world. And a god to put your faith in."

"Thank you."

Nisrine had her god; she did not have all her freedoms. I had my freedom.

"I want to add on to mine," I said. "I wish that for you, too."

INTERVIEW

ADEL'S FATHER HAD TOLD HIM, *You're a policeman, you can always do something.*

These were the things Adel could do:

He could knock on the door and ask for Madame: he had watched Nisrine with this family, he knew who the real trouble was.

Policemen didn't involve themselves with families.

He could come to Nisrine's rescue some other way, a fire hose like they'd once joked about. Find her money (what money? his mother's?).

He could do nothing.

Qais had done nothing.

He did what he could.

At the end of the week, Adel went down to the basement where he did his questioning. He watched the line of ex-prisoners each take a number from the red dispenser. He didn't call the next one in line from his steel desk, he called out of order. Baba sat down in front of him. Adel measured and weighed him, like a nurse at the hospital, and rewrote his physical description as he always did, to make sure Baba had not paid someone else to come in his place.

"Work?" Adel asked.

"Bookbinder," Baba told him.

"People seen?"

"Too many."

"People seen?" Adel asked again.

"Mohanad al Hasbi."

"Context?" said Adel.

"His house, a small party."

"Others?"

"I didn't know many at the party."

"Others?" said Adel.

"Haisam Marwani."

"Family?" said Adel.

"My brothers were there with me."

"Business?" said Adel.

"We're in bookbinding. I own a small factory."

"Immediate family?" said Adel.

"What?"

"Immediate family?"

"I don't know what you mean."

"Wife?" said Adel.

"Don't you talk about my wife."

"Wife, son, daughters. Servant!" said Adel.

Baba stood up. "I said it once. I'll say it again. I come here, I answer your questions. Don't you talk about my wife, don't you talk about my family."

"You have one servant," said Adel.

"She's like family."

"Sit down!" said Adel. "We're not finished."

Baba sat back down.

"Wife?" said Adel.

"You asked me about my business. I told you, we bind Qurans. You asked me where I went. I told you, a party. You asked about my brothers, I told you about them, too."

"Wife," said Adel.

Baba kicked the steel table. It made a deep ringing.

"Servant," said Adel. "Where has your servant gone? She went away, where did you send her? She came back two hours later, and your wife hates her. What has she done to deserve this?"

"Get me a man," said Baba. "You are not a man, I won't talk to you. Get me a man, I'll talk to him."

"Sit down," said Adel.

Baba sat down. Adel hit him.

"That's right, hit me." Baba stood up. "You're not a man. Hit me again."

Adel felt himself grow large, his head and heart expanding. He hit Baba again. Baba sat down hard, as if the hit hurt him.

"Servant," said Adel.

"I don't have any servants. My wife does."

"Nisrine," said Adel. "What have you done to her? She's miserable, she wants to leave, what have you done?"

ADEL WAS ALWAYS MOVING. In his stories, he was always jumping up on his toes, or sitting down against the wall to show something: How he hugged his mother. How, when they found out about his accent, the border guards teased him. When he talked to Nisrine, he wanted her to hit him, hard, like the police did, because he wanted to feel her hands on his stomach. Of course, she wouldn't, she couldn't reach from across the balcony.

Hit me, Nisrine! Hit my belly!

After the fight, Adel went up to the rooftop. Blood was pulsing. His mind raced. He called his mother. The interview kept playing in his head, his hand against Baba.

"Mama, have you ever seen a fight?"

"Yes."

"How'd you feel when you saw it?"

"Disgusted."

"You got a really sick feeling, didn't you, when you saw that fight?"

"Yes."

His hand, today, against Nisrine's kind Baba.

"You're right, I don't like to fight."

"You don't?"

"You get that sick feeling when you're in the fight, too. Not at first. At first there's a lot of adrenaline and you're going to beat the guy. But afterwards. It seems pointless and you get that sick feeling."

His mother sighed. "Well then, Adel, don't fight."

What else could he have done?

He remembered her when he had first met her, the perfection of her lips, her little hand when she gave him apples. He had loved that hand first, later the rest; it had once brushed his, the closest he had come to touching her.

She would be in more trouble now, once the family found out. What could he do for her?

He thought of their joke, *Run away with me?* in her high voice. They *had* been joking, hadn't they?

On the phone, his mother waited. "Adel? I said, don't fight."

The blood that had filled him slowly left. Fear, like butterflies, replaced it.

"It's just, sometimes you have to fight. You're in love, she's in trouble, you have to do something."

JAIL

"DOGS," BABA SAID when he got home, and he meant the police. "They get the stupidest men to interview you, really. They treat you like a donkey. Animals!"

The children and I were eating in the kitchen. Madame had prepared us yogurt. Nisrine was in the hallway, dusting. Baba jumped on me, as if I had done something.

"You foreigners think everything is so easy. You think you can befriend anyone you want, and butt in anytime, and it doesn't leave consequences."

I didn't know what he meant. I didn't know where I'd butted in.

"You know, anyone who has done anything in this country has worked and they have suffered for it. There aren't friendships without consequences, here. There isn't work without suffering. I know a cultured man with three books and they decided to call him for his army service. A cultured man and he was called away in his prime to be treated like a dog. But he didn't give up. He came back, and he wrote some more and then they exiled him. His father died and he couldn't come back to see him. This was his reward, for persevering. I have a friend—Amal knows him. He was jailed last week. He posted on the Internet. You think I can have a business like my factory and not suffer for it?"

"No, Baba, I don't think you can."

"I suffer for it."

Madame said, "Don't yell, Hassan. Bea hasn't done anything to you."

"But she liked a policeman, didn't you, Bea? She's so in love with a policeman, she can't see the problems it causes. She thinks our police are like hers. She doesn't know their history."

I felt a sinking feeling. "I'm sorry, Baba."

Baba wasn't interested in sorry.

"There was a massacre up north. You know my first wife was from the north? The army came in and burned her town. It's on a river. Even the river looked like it was burning. After that, we all had to recant. We had to sign a statement and give ourselves in, but of course no one wanted to give himself in, and so they jailed us. Even the ones who recanted, it didn't matter, they jailed them. Just like now. The police, Bea, the ones you think are pretty, they jail men. You think there's a resistance? There's no resistance. The police jailed or exiled or killed all the resistance. They killed anyone who thought. There are young boys now, but they have no experience and no plan. The president, he knows who they are, he makes friends with their friends. He puts them in jail for six months or a year and when they get out, their political career is done. They don't want anything to do with politics after that. They just want to have a family and eat and live in peace. It's humiliating. They treat you like a dog, it's humiliating."

Madame said, "Then quit, Hassan. Quit, and live in peace. Don't be humiliated."

"It doesn't matter, I must continue. It makes the small things very important, doing them here. Very important!"

Baba brought his fist down on the table and accidentally hit my cell phone.

"Ow," he said. He lifted his hand. The phone's screen was cracked. There was blood on one side.

Madame said, "Hassan, look what you did."

I said, "It's OK."

Baba was holding his hand.

"I'll fix it. Here, Bea, see if it still works."

Madame circled the table to stir garlic into each of our yogurts. She handed me a napkin and I wiped the blood off my phone. It no longer had a dial tone. She handed Abudi a piece of bread.

Baba said, "There were two hundred of us in one room in prison. There were holes in the walls, and they were not covered with glass, and there was no heat, so when it was cold, we were cold until God warmed the weather. Do you hear that? Until God warmed the weather! And here you think you have a gas problem. In the ceiling, there were two holes where light came in. The light was always on. When I first came, they told me, 'Take off your clothes,' and they beat me. I was number seventeen. Of course, they learned the techniques from America and Germany—are you listening, Bea? Your country that's so high and mighty, it's butting in, it's imposing sanctions. Sanctions don't hurt the government, they hurt the people.

"A nurse came in and wiped off the blood. There was blood in my underwear. He had to lift my underwear. Then they put me back in the room with the two holes for light, and I was quite happy, I thought, Here I am, there's no beating and there's light. You see how low were my expectations! I thought those two holes were sunlight and I was happy about the light, but they weren't. It was artificial light and the guards looked down on us from the holes and that fake light, so we couldn't move without them knowing, if we moved they would pick us out. The general would watch with the guards from up above. He'd say, 'You see that man?' The next day, they would call that man out and beat him, and then two of them would throw him back in to us. Of course, we had no way to clean him. We would rub his blood off for him with our hands. Eat your yogurt, Abudi."

Madame said, "You're excused, Abudi. Go play in the living room."

Baba said, "There aren't death certificates for the ones they killed. Of course, I know who they killed. But there aren't certificates. Of course, that's a problem now, because the deeds of their houses and their shops and cars are in their names, and you can't change those over to their children or wives until the government sees a death certificate, and of course there's no death certificate. Their wives can't remarry."

Madame said, "Lucky wives!"

Baba nodded at Madame. "She came after my trip," he told me. Meaning, he married her after jail.

"Lucky me," Madame said, "lucky for your first wife you came back, so she could remarry."

"God provides for us," Baba said.

Abudi came running in. He said, "Bea, Nisrine is taller than you are!"

Nisrine was on a ladder in the hall, cleaning the ceiling. I could tell by her face she had been listening.

Baba looked at her. He said, "She's my problem."

We all looked where Nisrine was. Until now, I had thought I was Baba's problem, I and my country. He had been talking to me.

Baba looked at Madame. "Don't get mad at her, Amal, it's not her fault. A policeman fought me and asked for her."

Silence. So, this was the problem. This was why Baba had come in, angry, mad at Americans who butted in, talking about the consequences of friendships.

Adel had fought Baba. I felt myself floating.

He had fought, and asked for Nisrine, but I had been the one who liked him first, everyone knew this, and I had been in the kitchen sitting before Baba, my country imposed sanctions without thinking, so Baba had talked to me.

We were all standing. Madame raised a hand, and for a moment, I thought she might run and hit Baba, or me, or Nisrine. I wasn't sure who. Then, she dropped her hand and sat down. She seemed very old in the chair. I saw all her wrinkles, like a balloon the air had gone out of.

Nisrine came down from the ladder.

"I'm sorry, Baba," she said. "I'll fix it."

Everyone should have been mad. No one was mad at the table. Baba wasn't mad anymore, he'd lost all his anger. He had been angry for all of us.

We four sat looking at one another, not knowing what to do. Finally, Madame said, "Nisrine, go do the ironing."

"I'll fix it." But, there was a brightness to her eyes. And all of a sudden, I realized: she had been wanting and asking and waiting. She was unhappy, in an impossible situation. She had asked Baba, she had asked me, we had done nothing—

Adel had fought Baba. He had done something.

Baba stood up. He said to Madame, "I'm going. You need anything?" His hand was still bleeding.

Madame roused herself. "Right now? Stay awhile, Hassan."

But Baba was already putting on his shoes. He said again to Madame, "Don't do anything to her, Amal. She's a good girl." He looked at me. "They both are. A policeman asked for her, we need her." Then he said, "Lema, get me my socks."

Baba had not said anything about it, but the air had changed, and we all had a suspicion about where he was going. Suddenly, the divide between us lessened; we all tried to keep him.

Lema rolled her eyes. She finished her yogurt, stalling. "It's as if he's my husband, not yours," she said to Madame.

"He's your father."

Lema brought him socks from the hall closet.

"Bea, what color are these? They look black. I don't want black socks."

I was still floating. I thought of Baba, being hit by a policeman. I thought of the policeman, asking and asking. I thought, like Nisrine thought, that he had not wanted to hurt Baba. Still.

Baba had been deciding whether to sign a document.

"My God, Baba," Lema said for me about the socks, "you really have a problem with your eyes. They're coal."

"They're coal. Put them on, Hassan," Madame said. "The winter socks are all packed away, you can't have them."

Baba put the socks on.

Madame smiled. "You see how he listens to me?"

But, only about socks. Not about staying.

"Because I'm stupid like a donkey. That's why I listen to you. Bea, give me your cell phone."

"It's OK, Baba." Don't go. Don't go, don't do anything rash, don't decide because of a fight to sign.

"Don't be silly, I broke it. I'll fix it."

He held out his hand, and I gave him my cell phone.

"I'm sorry, Baba."

Madame said, "Remember us, Hassan. Before you do anything, walk awhile and remember us."

He asked Madame, "You need anything?"

And I could have thought of several things:

Baba safe, Nisrine safe, Adel safe, a new cell phone, none of this to have happened, we must talk to Adel, before Baba signs, Nisrine must talk to him—

Madame shook her head. "No, Hassan. Your health."

AFTERWARDS, we watched one another in silence. For a long time, Madame had suspected. Now, she knew out in the open, but Baba had made her promise not to do anything. So, she just watched.

For Baba, it had been easier to blame me, because I was American; in blaming me, he could educate me about America. For Madame, it was easier to blame Nisrine; she was the maid, Madame had already blamed her for so much, and now it turned out that blame was just.

Before, Madame had not wanted to be in the same room as Nisrine. Now, she didn't want to let us out of her sight, she didn't know who we would run and talk to. So, we all sat together in the kitchen, watching the light fade out the window, until eventually Nisrine couldn't sit anymore, and she went to do the ironing in the hall where Madame could still see her. Through the dusk, her eyes shone like stars.

My head was busy with things we should be doing, policemen we should be calling, fixing. Madame watched us.

After a while, she said, "We had trouble before, this isn't our first trouble. I remember when foreigners entered our neighboring country. There were foreign tanks and everything in the street, and checkpoints. Like now, except there were so many more checkpoints. We lived like that for ten years, next to the foreign army."

I said, "That must have been very hard."

She shrugged. "Militias rose up and pushed the foreign army to the south, and there were rumors that the foreigners would leave. Lema was one and a half years old. I had a friend living in the south, so I went there, just to look at the foreign soldiers, to see what they looked like before they left. It was cold out, so cold, I remember, and everyone here was scared for me. They said to Baba, 'How can you let your wife go and do that? And take your child?'

"Coming back, in the taxi we were scared. The situation had gotten worse, you see. It was cold, so cold. We waited five hours in the garage for the car to fill up. The driver wouldn't leave without a full car, the donkey. After five hours, we had three passengers and I told him, 'You'd better hurry up and go. Three's enough,' I said. So we went, it was so cold, and we kept getting stopped by the foreign soldiers at checkpoints along the way north. I remember one looked at Lema and made a joke about her. They knew some words in Arabic—'open the window,' for example. They did bad things to our neighbors, they helped massacre people. But I was looking at them, and looking at them. I thought they were so beautiful!"

Beauty. Men in foreign uniforms, whom you know it is wrong to like, and yet you do.

"I understand Hassan," Madame said. "Me, I like to look, I like to be involved. But I'm not like Hassan, I don't stay. I don't sign my name. A day or two, and I want out."

I came to stand beside Madame at the window. It was dark

now. We looked over the city, to the road like a black river; to the white glow of TV screens, strung together from apartment to apartment, like Christmas lights.

"Mama, what will happen to Baba?"

"I don't know."

"Do you think he'll really sign the document?"

"I don't know, Bea, I don't know."

"Maybe we can fix it."

She gave me a long look. "Don't try to fix anything."

But, so much in me wanted to. Adel, I thought. Adel, who had done something. Could he really have fought Baba? I felt the secret care I'd harbored for him for so long slowly melt away; all at once, Imad was there instead. Imad, who had traveled all over England; who'd never hit anyone, that I knew of. Imad, who knew all about how to work with foreigners, which drew me to him, but made him suspect for the police. His kisses had come like thank-you notes, strung out after a long time behind our studying. He was not Qais. Still. Tomorrow I would see him, and we'd go together before his interview to the National Library, and this time maybe Imad would help me, maybe with him I'd finally read the astonishing text. I had dreamed about crying over that text for so long, and now all of a sudden I didn't know whether I wanted to cry for the text's beauty, or so that Imad could comfort me.

"Mama, did you have boyfriends before Baba?"

"Yes," Madame said, "I had lots of boyfriends."

"Who was your first?"

"The neighbor, when I was thirteen."

"Who was your longest?"

"They were all very short."

"How did it last with Baba, then?"

"We made a choice, we had to stick by it." Madame was married when she was twenty-three.

Lema had come in while we were talking. She stood behind us, listening. "Is marriage hard?" she asked.

"Very hard. Even though I loved Hassan, there were a lot of times I thought of leaving. But, I made a choice."

I thought of Baba, nights when he came home and we were so happy to see him. I thought of him in jail in a room without sunlight.

"Did your marriage with Baba succeed?"

Madame didn't answer for a while. Then she said, "Yes, it succeeded."

"Do you still think about leaving?"

"No, now it's much easier because it's become normal. Everything is normal."

"Have you ever loved anyone after you loved Baba?"

"No, of course not. That is all done."

In my head, I made exchanges: All the words I knew, for Baba's safety. All the books in my drawer, for this to be all right.

Lema asked, "Mama, why did you choose Baba? He didn't have anything when he came to you. He'd just got out of jail."

"His family lied to me. They said they would give him both factories, and money. But they didn't give him anything. He had to earn those for himself."

Lema asked, "What's your favorite thing about Baba?"

We were always so anxious for him. We waited for him in the evenings, and never wanted him to leave. And now, the document. I looked at Madame.

"What did you say, Mama?" She'd said a word I didn't understand. She said it again. Then she said, ". . . and his patience."

I was here to read an astonishing text.

I'd studied so many words for love in Arabic.

Her favorite thing about him was a word I didn't understand.

THE WOMEN STAY, and the men go, and we don't know how to help, we don't know what to do.

Madame and Lema and I sat in the kitchen a long time, while Nisrine ironed. When it grew late, Madame went to put Dounia and Abudi to bed, and that is how she found my big bag beside Nisrine's mat on the floor in the bedroom, where we had once wheeled it, for when Nisrine could leave. She dragged it into the hallway.

"Bea, are you going somewhere?"

"No."

Madame said, "I thought this bag was yours."

Nisrine stood watching. "It's mine."

I said, "I gave it to Nisrine, to put her clothes in."

Nisrine and I had both loved and talked to a policeman, and so we were both to blame, though only one of us was loved back.

Madame talked only to me. "You don't have to do that. I'm in charge of her. I can buy her a big bag."

"It's OK, I wasn't using it."

"I'm in charge of her. I was going to buy her a big bag next year, when her contract is up. But, here it's in the way. The children can't get to their closet."

I went with Madame to drink water from the bottles that we had filled before bed. In the hallway, the ironing sat in piles, and the iron balanced neatly on its board, where Nisrine had left it.

Madame gave me her bottle to hold. "Look, Bea, it's still plugged in, do you see that? She's dangerous. She wants to kill us. First the gas, then this." She unplugged the iron.

I said, "It was off. It was plugged in, but it was off."

"You don't understand because you don't have children. Maybe someday you'll understand. I have a responsibility to be safe. You see how before we eat, I wash the parsley with iodine? That's to kill the toxins, to be safe, they put sewage on the parsley, they irrigate with sewage here. I don't know when I'm not looking if she really washes the parsley, or maybe sometimes she mistakes iodine for bleach, I don't know with her anymore. I can't trust her." Madame shook her head. "You don't have children, Bea. You don't know what it takes to build a family, and then some stranger comes and messes it up."

Madame had wanted Nisrine to leave. She had complained ever since she and Baba brought her back. But, she wanted Nisrine to leave on her terms.

Nisrine had loved a policeman, and he had fought Baba, and this, we worried, had been the last straw, it decided Baba about the document. If he was going to fight, then it would be for signing, something he was proud of.

Madame found she could do nothing about this. Adel had fought because Nisrine wanted to leave, and now Baba had gone to sign, which meant he would be in more danger.

It was not just Nisrine's fault: if Baba signed, that was his choice, not hers, not mine, not Adel's.

About a bag, Madame could do something.

I helped Madame drag my bag back into our bedroom and put it high on the top shelf, where you needed a ladder to get to it, for next year, when Nisrine's contract was up and she could leave.

WE DID NOT TRY to talk to Adel; Madame was watching. Though I wanted to, I did not try to talk to Nisrine.

That night, I dreamed of Imad. In my dream, we were both in America, where Imad fit in and spoke perfect English. Here, I stood out with my messy hair and loose jeans, but not Imad. He dressed perfectly and, as I dreamed, he grew with my culture, like Qais who grew into the name Crazy for Leila, or like the small scar on my finger that I got from a scissors when I was young: separate, but a part of me.

I woke in the middle of the night to Baba's hand on my shoulder. "Bea, phone call."

So, he had come back to us. He smelled of smoke and old men.

I untangled myself from Lema's legs and followed Baba, soft as dust, down the hall to the living room, where he handed me the house phone. My father was on the line. He'd tried my number and couldn't get through. He didn't call often. He didn't realize that here, it was two a.m.

On the phone, my father said, "How are things, Bea?"

"Fine."

Baba sat down across from me. In the dark, his hunched back looked like a lone mountain.

My father said, "Your mother says you're thinking you might come home early."

I had been thinking about it. But when he said it, I suddenly didn't want to admit this to him. "Well, there's that reunion."

"That might be a good idea. It sounds like your mother wants you to come home."

I sat near Baba in the dark living room with my legs curled under me. In the United States, my father was making dinner. I could hear him slice tomatoes and grate cheese. I couldn't remember the last time I'd had tomatoes with grated cheese. I closed my eyes and tried to pretend I was in the United States, with my father. I tried to listen past his words, to the sound of the grating.

He asked, "Why so silent tonight? Is everything OK, Bea?"

If I wanted, I could describe every move my father was making as if I were standing next to him; I'd spent every summer since I was small with him, and I'd watched him make dinner a hundred times this way. But he wanted to talk about how far away we were from each other, and did I miss home? He missed me, did I miss him? So, I stopped pretending we were close and there were no countries between us, and instead I sat on the sofa knowing I was speaking to my father out of nowhere, because he had no idea what this sofa or this city looked like, he would have no idea about what to do with a maid who was unhappy, or a policeman, or a document calling for an end to censorship and free elections; he wouldn't understand these things, like he didn't understand this city.

When I hung up, Baba said, "You're going to leave us, Bea?"

I didn't know what I was going to do. I wanted to ask Baba if he had signed.

I opened my mouth, but he said, "Amal wants me to leave."

"She does?"

"She's worried about my interview. She thinks I went too far, I insulted a policeman." He didn't mention Nisrine's and my connection. "I go to the Journalists' Club; this, too, is dangerous—it's a place for resisters, where we keep the document. Amal worries the police will find this place, I might be taken. I have a sister up north who said I could stay."

North, the place where they had once burned a river.

"Will you go?"

"Here are my people, I stay with my people."

Silence. All around us were dark blobs, the signs of disorganized life at Madame's. Crumbs like black dots on the end table, a pile of laundry, two tea glasses not in the sink. These were such small, ordinary objects to surround us. They felt like charms. With a pile of undone laundry beside us, how could Baba ever be forced to leave? I closed my eyes, and hoped to charm away trouble.

I thought, Maybe Adel can still help. Maybe there's still time.

Baba said, "You don't talk much about your father, Bea. What does he do?"

"He works in a bank. My mother's a veterinarian."

Baba nodded. "I like animals. Amal doesn't, though."

I already knew this. Madame was always complaining about stray cats that got in.

Baba said, "You know Amal was engaged to my brother?"

"She was?"

Baba nodded. "When I went to jail, he took over my business, but he was a profligate. God provides for us. When I came back, he'd ruined my business, and he liked many women."

"So, what happened?"

"God sees everything."

I didn't understand.

"He was young and liked women. Forty days after I came back, they took him to the hospital and he died."

"God rest him," I said.

"God rest him."

Baba said, "Amal was very in love with him. Her identity card was written in his name. He was in love with her, too, and when he died I brought her the identity card and all the papers, and I told her he had passed away, and then we began to talk and later I asked if she would like to marry me instead, and she accepted."

I thought of Madame, who liked to skin good meat; who boiled milk, then chilled it to separate the cream, but wouldn't let anyone eat it, because it was fattening; who gathered all the children together to suck the marrow from the bones when she cooked them; who put one bone aside in a plastic bowl for Baba to suck, even though it was cold when he got home. I asked, "Are you and Mama happy together, Baba?"

"We're happy. Amal saved my life. When I came back from jail, I had nothing, no one. She gave me something to set my heart on, to make me feel whole. We've created our own language together." Their own language. I wondered what it was, how they came to decide on certain meanings.

Love: something to set your heart on.

Baba got up. "Well, it's time for bed." He picked up the tea glasses to leave in the kitchen.

I asked Baba, "You know your interview—"

He looked at me. "He's a donkey, Bea. Remember that. Police are all donkeys. Nisrine should, too, she should remember."

I nodded.

He patted my arm, then sighed. "It doesn't matter, it's nothing. I've been to jail."

It was nothing. Today you were here, tomorrow you took a plane and it all became nothing. Except, Baba and Nisrine couldn't just decide to take a plane, only I could.

"Baba, did you sign the document?"

"Yes."

Silence. After a while, he said, "It's not the interview's fault, Bea. I was going to sign, anyway. I have to, to keep my honor."

Honor, that word again. I had always loved Nisrine and Baba because they were brave, and stuck by their honor. But, I was beginning to realize the sacrifices behind bravery. Sometimes, honor isn't a blessing; sometimes, it comes between you and your family; or you, and all that you love.

"Bea, Bea, Bea," Baba said. "Did you know your name has a special meaning?"

"It does?" I knew my name as a preposition: on, or around, or in.

Baba nodded. "In," he said, "as, 'In the name of God,' the first word in the Quran." I was not particularly religious, but I respected religious books. Baba continued, "The Quran is a circular text. That means it keeps returning over and over to the same important points. There are some scholars who say its whole philosophy can be summed up in its first word. *Bea*: in, inclusive. It evokes a presence with God and the world, a sense of togetherness."

I stared at Baba. I loved Arabic for its meanings, but I had always thought my name was unimportant. Now, Baba had given it special significance like a new present, or a hidden world. *Togetherness*. I wanted to live up to my name in this house.

Baba asked, "Have you heard of the poem 'A Garden Among the Flames,' Bea?"

I had. It was the last poem I had read with Imad, about a man's green heart.

He nodded.

"I'm not surprised, it's quite famous. I know this isn't the most popular way to look at that poem, but I always thought of the garden as a blessing, and a curse."

"Why's that?"

"The man finds his heart is a garden, but you know he had to go through flames to get to it."

I thought about Baba's flames: jail, his lost first family.

I asked, "Do you have a garden, Baba?"

He looked around him. "This is my garden."

At Madame's, we rarely showed affection to men. I had made trouble, here; I had talked to a policeman, and it had led to a fight.

Now, I did what I could. I leaned over and gave Baba a big hug; I could feel the bones of his back through his stiff shirt.

He patted my shoulder. "Thank you, Bea. That means a great deal to me."

It was such a small thing, not even words of encouragement. But it did to me, too.

I remember the first week I lived at Madame's, Baba got his gallbladder removed. He left in the morning. Afterwards, he brought the gallbladder home in a plastic cup for Dounia to play with. It still had its wet blood.

Madame talked about how she wanted to have surgery on her leg next.

"If I did, I would make them put me to sleep. I couldn't do it watching like Hassan did."

After his gallbladder surgery, Baba kept pacing around. He did the dishes.

Madame said, "Hassan, *must* you tire yourself by pacing? Go lie down," but he wouldn't.

Of course, Baba didn't need to be put to sleep. It is nothing to watch them remove your gallbladder when you have been tortured for ten years. I thought about what Baba once told me, that after jail he knew he could live through anything.

A half hour after coming home from surgery, he didn't need to rest; he paced around and did the dishes, his resiliency the blessing and curse of a man who could live through anything.

Of course. He was always going to sign the document.

I DIDN'T GO BACK TO BED with Lema. I sat up watching the window until Baba fell asleep, wondering how much trouble he was in, and if I should make a plan. Trying to think of one. I needed to talk to Nisrine.

Eventually, I took the cordless phone to the kitchen and, even though it was very late, I called Imad.

"Arabic Hair," Imad said when he answered. This was becoming his nickname for me.

"Were you asleep?" I asked. "Did I wake you?"

"Yes. It's OK, though, I'm glad it's you. For a moment I thought it might be Security."

We both laughed. On the phone this late, his mistake seemed very funny.

Imad asked, "What is it, Bea? You can't sleep?"

"No." I wanted to forget about Baba, forget about what happened, for a moment.

"Imad, tell me more about the astonishing text. What was it like when you saw it?"

"Beautiful like you, haha."

"Haha, right."

I sat with the phone close against my ear, feeling the warmth of Imad's voice trickle down into my cheeks. I liked his little jokes, they helped me to forget. I liked that he complimented me.

I pretended not to. "Come on! What was the text like? Do you think I'll cry when I see it?"

"I don't know, Bea. That depends on you. It has gold vines around the edges."

"It does?" Gold seemed beautiful.

"And flowers in the center that are perfectly symmetrical, like a pretty face."

I let the phone lie. There was a warm, sleepy feeling coming over me, through my thighs and toes and breasts. I ran a finger through my hair, which curled like Leila's hair.

"What else?" I said into the phone.

"What else, what else . . ."

I could hear Imad thinking.

"How would you kiss Leila?" I asked him.

"How would I kiss Leila? I don't know, in her hair and ears and mouth, I guess."

"And then?"

Pause. "Am I alone with Leila?"

I looked around at the empty kitchen.

"Yes, pretend you're alone with Leila."

"Down her neck and her chest, and below her chest, then."

"And how would she move?"

"With her breath first. I would feel her breath catch."

"Would she like it?"

"I don't know, Bea, would she like it?"

There was a light airiness inside of me, like Imad's breath.

"Yes. And then?"

"I would run my hands along her lap, and put my head on her thighs."

"And then?"

"She would breathe like you're breathing."

"And then?"

It was growing and growing.

"She would feel what you're feeling."

I liked what I was feeling.

"My Arabic girl," Imad said, over and over. "My Arabic Hair. Do you like your hair, Bea? You should."

I didn't always like my hair. I liked what I was feeling.

"Where else would you kiss her?"

"All over, Bea. All over."

"Until she cried out?"

"Until she cried out."

Afterwards, I ran my fingers through my hair like Imad might, and touched my warm cheeks. We stayed on the phone in silence, listening to our breathing.

Imad said, "You'll see, Bea. It's a beautiful text. No matter what you expect, it surprises you."

"In a good way?"

"Sometimes in a good way."

How did I want to be surprised? I thought I might not care, as long as it made me cry. All this time at Madame's, I'd tried not to cry; I'd been saving my tears for that text.

"Imad, has there ever been a person who you loved, and worried about?"

"Of course, all the time. What's the matter? Is someone in trouble?"

I thought of all the people I cared for and worried about, including Imad now, with his interview. And Baba, and Nisrine. What would happen to us?

Imad said, "It's late, we should go to bed. Good night, Bea, don't worry, it'll be OK. I'm glad I'll see you tomorrow."

"Good night, Imad, I'm glad, too."

I hung up, thinking of gardens among flames, but not Baba's cursed part, only the green beauty. Imad was becoming one of my gardens. I went to him when I felt sad or worried, and he made it right. We had studied so many words for love in Arabic, he and I, across our classical poetry. Shouldn't I then love him, too?

I put the cordless phone back in its place, then tiptoed quietly to the children's room, where, sure enough, Nisrine was wide awake in the dark. She rose when she saw me; the two of us moved like light back to the kitchen.

Nisrine spoke first. "I talked to him, Bea." Her voice was clear and full; she was no longer distracted, no longer forgetting Arabic. "He did something for me. He fought, because he loved me." I felt a familiar cold. He had fought, and we had done nothing.

But, he had fought Baba.

I asked, "What will you do?"

All night in my head, I had been making plans: to talk to him, tell him how he must help Baba. Or better, not to talk. Never to talk again—

"He wants me to leave," Nisrine said.

There was a moment of silence.

"He says if I run away, he'll find me a new house to work in, so I can send my child money."

He was a young policeman.

He had fought for the woman he loved; it seemed now, he could do anything.

I had come to the kitchen to make a plan with Nisrine that involved not talking to Adel, not leaving with him.

"What about your child?"

"I'll be in a new house. I'll send him money."

Her eyes were so bright. In her voice was so much clarity. All it took was someone who stood up for her to bring it back. For so long, I had been trying for Nisrine to stay.

She said, "Don't you have your lesson tomorrow? I'll slip out with you, when you go to your lesson."

"Tomorrow?" It seemed so soon, tomorrow. Couldn't she wait a bit? Then I thought, It's not soon, if Baba's in trouble.

"He said tomorrow you should meet him?"

"He'll wait for me on the corner."

"He'll find you a new house?" She had her contract, her hidden passport.

"He'll find a new house."

"He won't bother Baba again?"

Why would he? She would be gone, he would know where she went. She could ask him to intercede, if Baba got in more trouble, she could talk to him.

What would Madame say if Nisrine left? But, Madame wanted Nisrine less now than ever. Baba and I both wanted her. The children wanted her.

Nisrine said, "I'll slip out just after you. We won't go together, so you don't get in trouble."

Despite myself, I was beginning to believe in this plan, even though it was sudden. Already, I missed her.

Adel had done something. The wrong thing, but still. If I helped her, would that mean I had done something for her, too?

"Make him help Baba, you have to."

She nodded.

We needed a solution.

She had talked to Adel, fixed things. I had been wanting to fix things.

"OK," I said, feeling the craziness of it all, the dark night, "tomorrow."

. . .

It was only after we'd hugged, said good night, and I'd slipped back into bed beside Lema that I remembered: Madame with my bag in the hallway.

You don't have to do that. I'm in charge of her. I can buy her a big bag.

My bag, with Nisrine's clothes, stashed high up in our closet where she couldn't get to it, placed there by Madame, who had complained for so long, but now didn't want Nisrine to leave.

LOCKED IN

THE NEXT MORNING after she found my bag, Madame was not talking to me. She locked the door even though we were all at home, and hid the key to keep us in and strangers out. She blamed it on Baba's revolution. "He angered a policeman," she said, not mentioning Nisrine. "There's no telling what will happen."

I was supposed to meet Imad in the afternoon, before his interview with Security, and Nisrine was supposed to run away to Adel, so we both woke early to prepare. I tried to take the garbage down to the street, but the door was locked.

I waited, holding the garbage, while Madame hunted and hunted for the key, not talking to me. Finally, she said, "Put it back, Bea. It doesn't stink. It can wait."

"Put it back?"

"Or throw it off the balcony, someone will pick it up."

"It'll land in the street."

"Someone will pick it up."

"I could just take it down to the corner."

Madame sighed. "Leave it, Bea. Eat your breakfast. We'll take it when I find the key."

Stuck in the house, the children became restless and moody, like Madame and me. Lema fought with her mother for a new swim-suit. She put on her jeans and threatened to leave, then took them off and wore her pajamas again, the whole time yelling at her mother, roaming around in her underwear, then her jeans, then her pajamas, then her underwear again, then her jeans. "It doesn't matter to me, someday I'll go home to my husband's house," she smirked, as if she were not only fourteen.

Nisrine and I conferred in the bedroom.

"What do we do? The door's locked."

We were not supposed to leave until the afternoon, though.

"There's time," she told me, and smoothed down a sheet.

In the living room, Lema dressed to go out. She tried to leave without saying good-bye, but the front door was still locked.

Madame fried eggplant for our breakfast. "She'd just leave?" Madame muttered about Lema. "Very nice, she'd just leave like that." She washed the parsley. She stirred the fava beans. She fried almonds. She poked at the eggplant.

Lema searched for the key, but she couldn't find it, so she shut herself in the bedroom. Madame cut parsley. She tasted the almonds.

After a few minutes, Lema came back out to the kitchen with a bright face and laughed and talked to everyone. She was making up to her mother by laughing and talking to everyone, except me, because her mother was mad at me. When she came to me, she pouted.

I sat at the table with the family, and all through breakfast there was an in-joke, and I was out. Madame and the children stuck together, laughing and talking, and they only stopped when they remembered I was there. They made jokes about feeding Baba coal if he didn't come home for dinner. Abudi took a raw eggplant from the counter and threw it in the air.

"Is that your dinner, Abudi?" I joked, but no one laughed because Nisrine was still in the bedroom and no one else was talking to me.

I gathered our tea glasses from the table to wash them, but Madame wouldn't let me.

"Go to sleep, Bea, you look tired."

It was only ten a.m.

"I'm not tired," I said, but no one was listening to me. They treated me like a guest. Madame told me not to clean up, but I did anyway, and it was a silent cleanup war.

"Leave those, Bea, you look tired."

"I'm not tired."

"Go to sleep, Bea."

I went to the bedroom and pulled the covers over my head, to be alone. I thought, Maybe I could lie here all day, until I went to Imad in the afternoon, and then I could come home from Imad and pretend I was sick and go back to bed and never get up again, and then I'd never have to see anyone. I began to worry for the first time about Nisrine's and my plan. Would it work for her to just walk out? I closed my eyes beneath the covers, and tried to imagine what it might be like if Nisrine left, but I couldn't; she was still of this place to me, the one I woke with in the mornings, who kissed me and each child before spooning out our milk. This was what she wanted. I tried to put myself in her place: What would I miss, if I were to leave? But, right then, I couldn't think of many things; Madame was mad, so I thought only of problems. Under the covers, I smirked like Lema. I had a family reunion. If I wanted, I could leave here right now, and then I wouldn't have to worry about Baba, or miss Nisrine so acutely, because I wouldn't be here either, we would both be gone, and so none of it would matter to me. Outside, the call to prayer sounded through the window, and even it was annoying, not pretty, and time loomed before me, and then even though I wasn't tired, I fell asleep.

When I woke it was afternoon, and there was nobody. Usually we'd eaten our big meal by now, but nobody woke me.

I dressed very quickly and walked down the hall to tell Madame I was leaving for class. Madame was nowhere. Neither was Nisrine. Neither were the children.

I wandered the rooms of our apartment, carefully opening the door of each one, and calling out. They must be somewhere. Madame never left the apartment, she was too busy. The children never left, because Madame worried when they were gone. I tried the front door, which was locked as always.

I wandered through the parlor and the kitchen, until I heard a voice in the children's bedroom. So that's where they were. It was muffled and low, as if the children were hiding under the bed. I set down my books, and began to walk very quietly to the bedroom, to surprise them. From the hall, I could see the door was closed. I would open it, and rush in. I rolled up my pants so they wouldn't swish, and crept silent as dust to the door—

"Bea? Is that you?"

The voice was Nisrine's.

I tried the door. It wouldn't open.

"Nisrine?"

"I'm locked in. Bea, is there anyone? It's the hour to meet Adel."

"Where's Madame?"

"She left."

"She left?"

Madame never left.

"Where'd she go?"

"Shopping."

She never went shopping.

"For Lema's swimsuit, Bea, you fell asleep. I've been calling and calling. I've been here for hours, I couldn't wake you. Why'd you fall asleep, Bea, I'm locked in, it's time to leave."

I jiggled Nisrine's door. It didn't budge. I pushed from one side, she pulled from the other. Still nothing.

"There must be a key," I said. I had class, Madame wouldn't lock us in when she knew I had class.

I ran to the front door; it was also locked. I tried Nisrine's door again. I called Madame's cell phone from the house line, but her cell phone rang in the kitchen. I called Baba's work phone, but he must have been at the Journalists' Club, where he said they kept the document, because his work phone kept ringing.

I went to the bedroom and pulled down the covers on all the beds to search for the key.

In the children's room, I heard Nisrine's soft movements. "Check the laundry," she told me from behind her door. I checked the laundry. "Check the bookshelf."

I said, "They can't just lock us in. There must be a key. She must have left a key."

From the other side of the door, I could hear Nisrine slowly exhaling. We felt the hazy afternoon. Time was passing. Through the door, she said, "Don't worry, you'll find it, Bea."

Over the next hour, I hunted all the places Nisrine and I could think of for the key, and instead everywhere I found dust and pills and creams. On the table in the kitchen. In the closet of Madame's bedroom. In my underwear drawer and Madame's underwear drawer, and on the stand by the sofa, where Baba put his wallet before he went to sleep. Madame had pills, and she had creams for every occasion, and she was always scolding the children with her cream half on and she was so busy having a maid and the children and me, that sometimes she didn't get to the other half of the cream, so her face would flake and turn brown. There was a cream for crow's-feet, and a cream to make big breasts, which she didn't need, coated with dust that clung around the edges despite Nisrine's daily sweepings, but no key.

I searched and searched. I ran back and forth before Nisrine's locked door, and she directed me. In the cupboard, with the turmeric. In the storage space beside the jam. I tore up drawers and closets, and only halfheartedly put them together again, rehiding the schoolbooks and trinkets. I looked between all Baba's newly printed bindings, and inside the children's outgrown shoes.

In the parlor was a picture of Baba with his first son when he was young, and Baba's hands at his sides weren't yet swollen like baby cheeks. I found a picture of Madame without her headscarf, holding Lema. I found a belt and the two bottles of perfume that I once tried to give Madame and Nisrine. I found that Lema had written a poem and received a teddy bear.

As I searched, I forgot how earlier in the day I had worried that if I left I would miss Madame's, and everything began to look to me like a sign of leaving: The garbage that went out in the morning had left us. The V's of the doves that Nisrine watched at the call to prayer, when we saw only their backs as they flew away. The shift changes on the roof of the police station. All these were small forms of leaving, and the garbage and the doves and the policemen did them every day without thinking, naturally, and no one got hurt.

I unfolded and refolded the laundry in search of the key. I

began to feel light like Madame's face when she put on new creams; pieces of me were flaking off and floating downstream, back across the ocean to where I came from. I thought up small ways, once Madame got home and this was solved, to get Nisrine out, and always be able to leave: How to go out for an hour to buy bread or tampons when we ran out of them. How to leave for two hours to see Imad and read the astonishing text. How to leave for days or even weeks with Imad on a vacation. I thought, This city has become hard, I need a vacation. But where would I go? I took out all the places I'd ever lived and tried them on: America with my parents, the university, Madame's. Every home seemed either lonely or stifling.

When I couldn't think of where else to look, I poured a glass of juice and sat before Nisrine's door in the hallway to call Imad and tell him I wasn't coming.

On the phone, Imad was disappointed.

"I was counting on seeing you today."

"I know, I'm sorry."

"I thought you wanted to go to the library together. I thought you wanted to read the astonishing text."

"I do, I'm sorry. I'm locked in."

"What do you mean, you're locked in? What about the father?"

"I can't reach him. He's at the Journalists' Club."

Silence.

I said, "I know, it's crazy. I'm sorry."

On the other end, Imad sighed deeply.

"Bea, you're a paying guest. Get a key."

I sat before the door on one side, and Nisrine sat on the other, and we watched light glint off all the buildings outside that were beyond our reach. Every now and then, I could hear her shift.

She said about Imad, "He'll come around. Don't worry. He's short with you because he wanted to see you."

The children's room door was thin. I tried again at the handle. "You push from the other side," but it was no use.

Silence. It had been a silly plan, anyway. How could she leave without a passport?

But, we had both been counting on it. I hadn't realized until now how much I, too, had begun to count on our plan, any plan.

Through the door Nisrine said, "I miss my child. You know when he was born, he cried and cried, and the only thing that stopped him was my pinky? He liked to suck on it."

Her child. What would become of him, if she left? Would she find a family and still send money like Adel promised? I thought of her, locked on the other side of the door. What would become of them if she stayed?

"Do you want a child, Bea?"

I wanted a child. Not now; now, I wanted a key.

"I miss my mother," I told her.

"I miss *my* mother. I miss my husband, and my nice life in Indonesia."

"I miss winter."

"I miss mangoes."

"I miss my warm house. In winter there's nothing better than a nice warm house."

"I miss sunsets, and sweet coffee."

"I miss drip American coffee, and my books."

"I miss Adel."

Pause. I told her, "Don't worry, you're going to see Adel."

"But not now. I was supposed to be with him now. He didn't mean to hurt Baba, Bea. You must know he didn't mean it. I miss touching him. He's never really touched me, only once, for a moment. I want him to run his hands up and down my shoulders."

Is it possible to miss something you've never felt?

I said, "I miss Imad's hands."

"Does he have nice hands?"

I thought of my own hands, and his voice last night through the phone. "He has nice hands," I said. "I miss the astonishing text."

"You've never read that text."

"But it's like you with Adel, I still miss it."

Through the door, I could hear Nisrine breathing. I closed my eyes and imagined the way she would sit: butt out, feet crossed. There are many kinds of intimacy. I knew all about Nisrine's small routines, the curl of her dark hair on our white porcelain sink. That hair had been an ache in so many ways, deep in my heart; but if she left, I would miss it, too.

"New plan," I joked, "cut a hole in the wall. Walk out when they get home. Tell Madame you have a date!"

Nisrine laughed. "I miss you, Bea."

And even though she was right here, only a door between us, I knew exactly what she meant. "I miss you, too."

For a moment, we were silent. Then she said, "Let Imad love you, Bea, it teaches you more than any text."

I thought about this, about how I had been trying to learn from a text for so long. I closed my eyes and tried to remember what I'd learned, but all I could think of was Nisrine's warm presence and then, unbidden, Imad's kisses.

And it occurred to me that Qais and Leila had never kissed; that the text I wanted to read, which was supposed to tell me all about love, was a text without kisses. Suddenly, I felt a great sadness for those ancient lovers, and all they had missed out on. I had always thought Nisrine and Adel were like Qais and Leila; of necessity, they lived with a faraway love. Before, this had seemed romantic, but now, locked here, I saw how it was a liability; how it limits love to rely only on words, poetry; for a moment, I saw all their love's imperfections.

"Nisrine, do you think you're like Leila?"

On the other side of the door, she was quiet, thinking. "I don't know," she said at last. "You know in that story I always wanted to be the shepherd?"

"You did?" So had Imad. Once, Nisrine had given me the role of shepherd. I was surprised. All this time, I'd been envying her the role of Leila, and here she was seeming to want what I had. "Why?"

"Because he came and went as he pleased. He stayed beside

Qais—I know it wasn't romantic love, but he could take Qais's hand whenever he wanted. Leila couldn't do that."

And then, I had an idea.

I ran to the balcony. Nisrine heard me leave—"What are you doing?" she called, but I didn't answer. I knew if my idea was going to work, we had to act quickly.

The balcony was bright with fresh air and busy streets. I leaned out, feeling the sun on my face, feeling policemen all around—

"Adel!" We could not call his cell phone, because mine was broken and the house phone wasn't for policemen.

"Adel, Adel!"

He wasn't on the roof; he had been down by the street like they'd planned, waiting for her. But, the other men heard me; one of them was dispatched, and soon enough a familiar face appeared.

I waved a greeting. We spoke in short sentences; sometimes the wind took them.

"Where's Nisrine?" he called.

"She's locked in."

"Locked in? Tell her to come, it's our day, I've been waiting!"

He was gold as ever, sunlight on treetops. I had not talked to him since Baba's interview, but it didn't matter. What needed to be said had already been thought in his direction. While I'd been locked in the house, my worries about him had fallen away.

And so, when Adel appeared on the rooftop I felt only hope, excitement.

From the children's bedroom, a window opened.

"Hello, *habibi*," Nisrine called, "we're locked in!"

He frowned. "Locked in?"

"Bea can't get to her lesson."

I saw his face fall. I thought, How will we fix this? They seemed destined to always be far away, never to cross the sky between them. Adel's eyes clouded—he had left her in a worse position, and in response, distraction and confusion rose from Nisrine's room.

Still, I had my idea. So, I measured the distance between us with my eyes. It was not far; the street was small, his roof and our balcony close to each other. Close enough, I had once thought, to throw an apple. Or, a man?

I looked around our small space. There was a clothesline behind me, a firm, thickish rope. I hung on it a moment. It held.

And, my actions seemed to give Adel the same idea. He said, "Bea, is that line loose?"

It was.

"Throw me an end."

I unhooked it carefully, while Nisrine watched from her window. There was blood pumping through us—what we were doing was daring, crazy, but it seemed to me then the worst had already happened.

I threw the rope. It made a straight line like an arrow from our balcony to Adel at the station. He caught his end, held it for a moment, considering. Then, he called his friends over; they stood on one side, I stood on the other, keeping the rope taut between us; my end was tied to the metal laundry hook.

He called to Nisrine, "If you can't get out, I'll come in!"

And with that, Adel did the second thing he had done for love:

he swung onto the rope until his feet hung five floors above the garden, and began to slowly make his way, hand over hand, to us.

There is a stillness to life five floors up, there is a slowness to time, when a man hangs, suspended like a small gold leaf, over a city. These were the dangers we faced:

That Madame would come home. That the rope would slip— Adel hung far above the world, even though our balcony and the roof were close. That his father would find out. Even if Madame didn't and his father didn't, the neighbors and the other policemen would see.

But, what did we have to lose?

We were already locked in.

Nisrine had already put her trust in this man.

We watched and held our breath. On my end, I felt the rope tense, the weight of it, the distance, as Adel's legs swung out, unhinged. He looked down on a view all his own.

He made his way slowly, sweat running down his face into his eyes and along his neckline. I saw the slippery way his hands gripped the rope. He hung by one arm in pursuit of his lover, who watched from her window and gasped, like I did, when for a moment he slipped, caught himself only with the help of his elbow. His legs traveled across my view of the sun.

But then he gave one last scissoring kick, and it was over, he had reached us.

I leaned down to clasp his hands in mine. He hung just below the rail.

"Help me up."

Earth rushed toward me, but he didn't need my help. He gave another kick and we both fell, one over the other, back onto the balcony.

We lay together for a moment, his legs on my legs, my head against his chest.

Then he stood up, offered me a hand. "Where's Nisrine?"

Her door was the next challenge. I brought him a knife and a hairpin to pick the lock. Neither worked. I brought him olive oil to ease the hinges. Finally, when that also failed, aware of the time and that Madame might come home at any minute, Adel beat on the door. He called longingly to Nisrine on the other side. He tore and jiggled with a lover's strength, until the handle came away altogether, the lock slid loose; the door swung jarringly open, and there she was.

I have never seen a lover of mine locked behind a door, and so I can only imagine what Adel felt. I think he was taken aback; he had dreamed of holding her close, but not under these circumstances.

Nisrine was beautiful, as always. Her veil had slipped off. It didn't matter what else had happened, when the door opened, she bloomed.

For a moment they leaned toward each other, drawn in the same direction like two flowers toward the sun. Then, Adel became shy, nervous—this was the most private place he had ever encountered her, and it was a bedroom. He turned abruptly, breaking the pulse between them.

"Let's get you out," he said, and ran to the front door, but here even his lover's powers failed him. It was thick wood, not made to be broken.

Nisrine and I stood to one side, watching. She reached out a hand to touch him on his back, then his chest as he worked, but it wouldn't budge. Finally, she said. "Leave it. It doesn't matter."

He cleared his throat. "How will you escape?"

It was clear Nisrine would not escape, today. She must face Madame and this family. But, there was still something she and Adel could do, another way to break the spell of faraway love. She took his hand.

"Come," and she tugged on him. He had been intent on the door, intent on his strength. There was not much time, Madame might be home any minute.

"Come, Adel!" she said again, and so he let himself be pulled by her; down the hall, through the living room, he left his tools. Two young lovers, they ran like light before me into the children's bedroom, where she turned, winked once, used both hands like birds on the unstable door, there was a scrape of wood, she pulled it shut.

For a moment, I felt bereft. Even though it had been my idea, they had gone and taken the excitement with them. I poured myself another cup of juice and sat in the kitchen, trying not to listen.

Outside, light glinted off the buildings where Adel had come from. Who had seen him suspended on a laundry rope like that, a straight line to our bedroom? The neighbors?

But then I glanced where Nisrine and Adel had gone; happiness spilled from their room, where, even though I wasn't listening, after a while I heard one soft giggle, like a perfect word.

AFTER LOVE

ADEL LEFT THE WAY HE HAD COME.

At the last second, Nisrine grew worried. "You must help Baba," she said. "Promise, he's signed a document. If he's in trouble now, you must help him."

He promised.

"And you must come for me." Madame would find out. When he swung over, the anticipation of love had kept them buoyant. Now, on the way back, they faced a precarious situation. What would happen to her? Madame would return her; she'd lock her in the closet.

"I'll come for you, Nisrine. I'll come for you tonight, tomorrow at the latest. I'll find you a new house."

He promised, too, that if he heard Baba was in trouble, he would send a warning.

She squeezed his hand, nodded.

He wanted her to go with him now; he wanted to swing her

like a princess across the rope. She refused. It seemed flimsy, dangerous. She would rather he get her at the door; until then, take her chances.

"I'll wait for you. But, Adel"—she looked for the birds—"I won't be locked in again."

On his way back he kicked out wrong, and there was a sudden sag of the railing. He let out a small cry, felt a sudden pain where his foot hit it, but it was only a moment. He swung hand over hand, with a full, expanded feeling. His head had grown to the size of a mountain, his heart burst in his chest. She was on every part of him: under his fingers, imprinted on the backs of his eyeballs.

At the station, he had missed his hour for questioning, so he had missed an interview with Imad. Another policeman had done it in his place. He went down to the basement, to read over what this policeman had written. As he read, his brow furrowed. There was troubling information.

Nisrine had told him, *You must help Baba,* and he had promised.

Adel paced back and forth. He was only one man, who had much to do that day—finish his shift, find a way to help Nisrine, find her a new family, come back for her. At the same time, his legs and arms felt soft as silk.

Police stations are like small towns, news travels quickly through them. The neighbors who might have seen Adel on the rope were not friends with Madame because they were on the side of the president, but they were loyal to the police. Adel's father was an important man, and so when they came to him, he did not waste time.

Adel was still in the basement. He looked up when his father entered.

"Who was your grandfather, Adel?" his father asked him.

"A general, may he rest in peace."

"Who is your father?"

"A general, may he live a long life."

"Who do you want to be?"

Adel had been asked this question many times. Before, he had always answered, *A general, God willing, like my father*. Now, he stopped to think.

His father didn't wait for an answer. "You were guarding foreign women."

"Baba, I'm in love."

"You rode a rope to see them."

"Baba, I've changed. Would you accept an Indonesian?"

"In this family, we don't change. When we do, it's for the better, we only change for the better."

Wasn't love better?

Adel's father hit him once, hard, across the face, the way Adel had hit Baba.

Adel stood up. "I'm a man. I love, and I'm a man."

Adel's father hit him again. Adel sat down hard, as if the hit hurt him.

"You know your grandfather was tortured? It was war, and foreign soldiers came to him. They wanted him to foreswear the president; they said, Change your words, change the president and the country you love. He said, I can't. So they hit him, until he was bleeding. From his head, he was bleeding. They said, Change your words. He said, What I speak is who I am. What I speak is right. Who are you, Adel?"

He was the grandson of a general.

"Who are you, Adel?"

He was the son of a general.

"Who will you be, Adel?"

There is a letter in Arabic that stands for silence. It is called the *hamza*; its shape is a half-moon, or a teardrop, and like a teardrop it asks you to pause a moment, and breathe. It opens up space.

Fighters will tell you that when they are in the middle of a fight, sometimes a strange thing happens. They cease to notice their pain and instead, they feel their souls open within them; they levitate. Some say it feels like love; others say this is the closest they have come to God.

Adel's father continued to hit him. Adel tried to stand. His face hurt. His side hurt. But his mind was a *hamza*, his arms open. His limbs from Nisrine were the softest flower—

"Who are you, Adel?" And his father wanted to hear, *A policeman*.

"Who will you be, Adel?" His father wanted to hear, *A general*.

But through his pain, all Adel could remember was a dark hip, a suprising feeling. He dug into this memory. He let it cover him.

"Nisrine," he said.

His father hit him again.

So, this was love. In the end, it was what you went to in your most painful moments, your darkest feelings. It lifted you, helped you to become another person, to know another side of yourself.

"Who are you, Adel?"

"Nisrine." He claimed her.

His father hit him over and over again, but Adel could only say her name.

I HEARD LATER that when it was done, Adel lay on his desk, unconscious. From the small window in the door, the other policemen stood watching.

Years before, when he was still a boy, Adel's father had taken his son up to their apartment roof and the two of them had looked out at thousands of stars like bright eyes. From his father, Adel had learned all the constellations.

Now, this same man looked down at his son on the desk. There was blood, and already Adel's face was turning a light blue-green riverish color. Adel's father stripped off his son's jacket; underneath was a policeman's vest; he stripped that off, too, until the young man lay small and boyish in his white T-shirt, like he had just gone to sleep.

Adel was a good height, but with a small chest, not as strong as a father might hope for. Still. On the desk lay Imad's interview, with the troubling information, and beside it, a poem. His father looked at the interview. He read it, then he read the poem, and pocketed them both.

He took his son in his arms and carried him home.

I might as well tell you now that Adel lay in bed for the next several days, while outside, worrisome events unfolded.

The first day passed. He was partway unconscious.

He could not call my cell phone, he thought it was still broken. Nisrine and I didn't know where he was. His phone had been taken by his mother.

A second day passed.

He should already have come for Nisrine, and in our apartment, the worst had happened. He did not know this, his mother wouldn't let him out of bed. She bathed his face and arms and, when he was awake, she sang to him.

A third, and a fourth day passed. On the fifth day, he got up and found that while he slept, his policeman's vest and coat had been taken.

He went to his mother.

"Mama, where are my clothes?"

His parents were having breakfast. They rolled their bread in small ovals like scrolls and dipped the round pieces in what they wanted.

His mother looked at his father.

His father looked at Adel. Adel's face was still bruised, when he walked he held it carefully. On his cheeks and ribs were red marks like precious stones. His father said, "What are you, Adel?"

He was a lover. However, he had learned his lesson. "My father's son."

"What else?"

"A policeman—"

His father shook his head. "Not anymore."

FIRE

When Madame came home, she was apologetic and no longer angry. "Why didn't you tell me you had class, Bea? I could have stayed here. It wasn't important."

She let me wash my own juice glass, and then Nisrine's, because she was no longer treating me like a guest. She didn't remark on the fact that Nisrine was in the hallway, instead of the bedroom where she had left her. She fished in her purse and drew out my cell phone, which was fixed and clean. She made Lema show me the swimsuit they'd gone shopping for.

That night, there was a commotion at the police station, but we couldn't tell what it was about. Afterwards, Moni called to tell us there had been a raid on the Journalists' Club, where Baba's document was, but the document had not been found.

Nisrine and I looked at each other.

If Baba was in danger, Adel was supposed to send us a warning.

We looked for Adel, but he had disappeared from our balcony, and he hadn't reappeared on the roof that night.

Secretly, I used my cell phone to call Nisrine's embassy, just to see what the options were for a maid without a passport.

A woman answered. She asked which family. I felt like a traitor. I wouldn't tell her.

She said, "Are they important?"

"Maybe."

She sighed very loudly. "Yesterday we got a call for three maids from an important family. You know, these people have so much money, and they just abuse them. Tell her to come to us, and we can help. But she has to come Sunday through Thursday, nine a.m. to two p.m. If she comes on Saturday, no one will be here." When I hung up with the embassy I called Imad, but there was no answer.

I went back inside and found Nisrine in the kitchen. "You can go to your embassy Sunday through Thursday, and they will help you—" I told her.

But just then, Abudi ran in to tell us a building was burning down the street. We stood at the kitchen window, watching the fire grow, and shook our heads at how long the fire trucks were taking. It grew and grew; Madame had been airing the house, and we rushed around closing all the windows so the smoke from the fire couldn't get in.

Madame called, "Look, look! It's spreading, it's not dying!"

We ran back to stand beside Madame at the window and watch the dogs and stray cats running out into the street from the buildings and the garden.

"Oh, how sad," Madame said. "How sad, how sad. It's spreading. Oh, it's spreading!"

I thought, If there were a fire here, we would all die because the door was always locked against Nisrine getting out and strangers getting in, and Madame could never remember where the key was hidden. I tried to decide if we could jump from the balcony, like Adel had. I thought about jumping from the balcony to save ourselves, now, often.

Nisrine and I moved about the house like careful ghosts, and we kept finding small evidence of the afternoon—a bookshelf, neat but not in order; a loose rung on the balcony rail. When we noticed these things, we quietly tried to fix them.

Madame came upon me.

"What are you doing in Lema's drawer, Bea, did you lose something?"

She went to hang the laundry, and found the balcony rail was loose.

"Come here, Bea. Did you see this?"

Adel had kicked the rail on his way back to the station.

I said, "I think it's been that way for a while."

Madame wiggled it. It swayed with her wiggling.

"It has? It's dangerous. It needs to be fixed."

We waited for Baba to come home, and Madame to find out, and Adel to come back. And the whole time, Nisrine was quietly glowing. She danced around the house, righting the mess I had made earlier, smiling to herself in the hallway.

For a joke, Abudi locked her in the parlor; she yelled and knocked determinedly, until he let her out.

I asked, "What was it like?"

"What? Love? Oh Bea, you'll feel it. It gives you hope."

Hopeful, we waited for Adel to show himself.

In the meantime, I was again part of the family. I counted for Dounia's jump rope. Abudi played games on my phone. Smoke hung like lace over our windows, obscuring our view so that our apartment floated high above, no longer part of the city, and this made me lonely.

I called Imad again and again, until finally he answered very politely, as if we were strangers and he hadn't been ignoring me.

"Do you need something, Bea?"

I asked, "How was Security?"

"They kept me an hour. I was late for my students."

"Did they take your license?"

"I kept my license."

Pause.

"Look, Bea, I have to go now. I'll talk to you later, OK?"

I asked, "Do you want to meet tomorrow? I can get out tomorrow."

"I'm busy tomorrow."

"When do you want to meet?"

Imad said, "I'm sorry, I'm feeling very strange from that interview. I'll call you sometime, OK? And we can start again."

We hung up. I concentrated on feeling angry, not sad. We'd only kissed twice. Lema had been standing in the doorway, listening.

She said, "Forget him, Bea. Don't worry. Matt *mat*. Haha. *Allah yerhamo*."

Madame came in. "What's the matter? Bea looks sad."

"I'm not sad."

Lema said, "Matt *mat*."

"Matt *mat?* Good riddance. Men, who needs them? You're better off without him, Bea."

WHEN WE WERE GETTING READY for bed, Baba came home in a rush, grabbed the TV remote from Abudi in the living room, clicked off the cartoons, and turned to the national channel.

"Open the window," he said, "open the window! Is there rain? See if there's rain."

On the TV, there was a mosque filled with men. They were praying for rain. Winter had gone and spring had come and there had been no rain since December, only fire and heat. They lifted their palms skyward, and the mosque looked thick with hard men's hands.

Madame and Nisrine and the children and I sat with Baba before the TV screen, watching the air out the window, feeling the warmth of Baba and the fire around us as we leaned out to see, beneath the burnt cooking oil and carpet smoke and car oil, if we could smell rain. When a few drops fell, we smiled.

THE POEM
ADEL'S FATHER
FOUND

To My Flower, the Jasmine. Written 25 April, by this poet-policeman, after the most beautiful of meetings. Amended after reading an interview with a tutor of Americans, to serve as a warning.

*Note: Nisrine, the poem is in blue. The explanation is in red pen beneath.

To My Flower, the Jasmine:
My heart is an occupied place.

You've occupied my heart.

And Lover, is the true title of those who love.

Lovers always know if their love is true.
Even if we make mistakes, that's OK, as long as you tell me.

In Love and Feeling, she is the best teacher.

You're a maid. You are in charge of the children's moral education. You tell them, Don't lie and swear. After the bathroom, Wash your hands. So you teach me in love. Because you're honest and pure. And when you love, you love truly. This is the first time I've said that to you, but I felt it. Today, I felt it. If we weren't in love, would we feel that?

And let me be among her wards.

Don't those children have to drink their milk? And don't you feed it to them? I want to drink it! Feed me like your children!

Because she is the most beautiful teacher,
And in strength, she won't be forgotten.

I can't forget you.

In our first words

When we first met

She was the one who offered.

You drove up to the station. You offered me apples.

And the children of the desert,

You know the children of the desert, they're the ones who've grown in the desert. But here, it means this city.

In a place no one enters but the weak.

Meaning the police station. Who enters the station?
Criminals and past criminals. What are criminals?
They're weak of morals, this makes them weak.

And the cruel, deranged.

In the prisons, you see a lot of cruel, deranged men.

And heaven's meek.

The criminals come to the station, and here they are
made meek. I'm describing the station to you.

And they ask, scared and humble,
Like all humanity, calling.

They are scared. They ask, Will I die here? Will I live
to be free? I'm describing the station. But I don't like to
say the word "station," so I describe it to you instead.

And in that place, in her offering,
I found happiness.

You gave me apples. My friends were going for
cigarettes. I told them, Cancel! Cancel! And I
watched you—What was your position? You were
sitting here. And Mohammed, here. And I came and
stood next to your car, and you should have given the
apples to Mohammed, he looked like the one in
charge because he had the most buttons, but you
didn't, you gave them to me, and your face was just
like a jasmine. I'm coming, Nisrine. Please believe
me, I'm coming. There's trouble. I read it today, in

the interview with Bea's tutor; he gave away Baba,
he gave information, did Bea tell him? Don't worry,
I've taken that interview, I'm going to hide it, but I
worry the police have already read it. If they come, I
will be with them, I'll protect Baba, like I protect
you. Wait for me, Nisrine, I can still feel your kisses,
they bloom inside me, I will always protect you, I
will always come for you, and I will never leave you.
I'm a policeman. I'm your policeman, I'm coming!

And, if only he had come. If only we would have seen this poem, had some news, some warning—of course, we didn't. Before Adel could send it, his father found it. It was only sent years later, without the interview, when Adel came upon it and, having a different view of words and poems by then, bundled all of them up together and sent them to the only person he knew who might still love them: me.

WE WAITED ALL NIGHT and the next day for him to come for Nisrine. A whole day was the longest Adel had ever been gone from the roof.

But, we were hopeful.

We didn't know what had happened, and so we said to each other, "It's taking a little longer, that's all." He had ridden a rope to see her. "He'll come."

SNOW

AFTER THE RAIN IT SNOWED, just as we thought spring was here. It never snowed in this city. It never snowed in April.

The snow came early in the morning and stayed until evening, a faint white dusting. On the news, they warned of death from the temperature drop. At Madame's, we all ran to the kitchen window to watch the snowflakes. Nisrine and I looked for Adel.

The children wanted to go down and see the snow. They opened the window and stuck out their fingers to feel it. Dounia opened another window and hit Abudi's head in her excitement, which made him almost cry.

To make up for locking me in yesterday, Madame let me take the children down to buy tampons and junk food. Nisrine helped us put on our hoods. Dounia whined for us to wait while she tied her shoes. We waited. Lema helped her. Madame videotaped us getting ready. Dounia waved at the camera and danced around like a snowflake. We crossed the street to the convenience store and asked for Tampax, and potato chips and gum. Then, we came straight back to the apartment because we knew Madame was watching, but Dounia didn't want to go in yet, she wanted to play longer in the snow. It was falling on our hair. It was falling on the balcony, and Madame's camera. It left dirty marks from the dust where it landed on Lema's white veil.

"Come on, Dounia." Abudi and Lema and I got in the elevator. Dounia stood outside looking at us. We closed the elevator door and rode up to the apartment without her.

Madame opened the door.

"Where's Dounia?" So Abudi went down to get her and bring her back up, while Lema and I shivered and giggled and stripped off our layers, cold and happy from the unexpected snow.

Nisrine found me in the hallway. "Did you see him?"

She meant when I was down in the snow, had I seen Adel? I hadn't. I had looked.

She sighed. "He'll come. Anyway, he promised to send a sign if there was trouble."

The snow came, and like the rain, it brought police. Moni called to tell us the police had surrounded our building. Nisrine and I looked at each other. Adel had promised to help her and Baba. Yesterday, those promises had seemed possible. Now, I took them out in the glare of the melting snow and looked at them again; could a young policeman do all this?

Madame sat silently at the table, sipping her afternoon coffee. First she drank her cup. Then she drank Baba's because he was too busy.

There was a knock at the door. The phone was ringing. In the living room, Baba, who had been to jail before and knew his whole life that at any moment the police might come again, put a finger to his lips to silence the children. He hunted in the closet for his passport.

"Lema," he said, "get your scarf." Then he called for Madame to get water and her scarf, too.

I said, "We'll help, Baba."

Nisrine stood behind me, pale but hopeful.

Moni called again. Another friend was also being taken.

"What do we do?"

"We get him out," and Baba, having just signed a document, holding his passport and wrists as if shackled in front of him, walked straight to the door while Madame in her veil and bathrobe prayed and sprinkled water for good luck behind him: he let the policemen in.

I have since dreamed of this day. The police came, and I did not understand all they were saying. They dressed in gray. They were tan skinned. Their pants sagged around their backsides, hid their butts but not their sweat. There were wet marks beneath their armpits, and it reminded me of Imad, or Nisrine when she'd been working. As I watched them sweat, I was aware of the fine points of bone in my crotch and my cheeks.

When I replay it all at night in my sleep, the police have batons, but in real life, they had guns. Every time that I had walked home from Imad's along the street, I passed the policemen and their guns. I passed the plainclothes officer who always stood before the garden. He hung his rifle from his neck with a sling for a broken arm, as if he had three arms to be broken. Sometimes as my gaze brushed him under the shadow of his weapon, I was aware of the same points in my cheeks; it meant they were reddening. Sometimes, I felt a pressure beneath my arm, and I thought it was his finger—whose finger? Imad's finger? Adel's gun finger?—or perhaps the pressure of his gun against the garden gate. This is the power of a rifle. You feel it in all the corners of your body. I walked past him and did not touch him anyplace he bulged, I did not touch him—

We stood to one side. Four of them entered. We waited for more, a blond head, a wide smile—

The last one shut the door.

Adel had not come.

Madame said, "Stay together," while Baba faced the policemen.

She wouldn't let the children wander off to the rest of the apartment; she didn't want them alone near the police. She refused Dounia when she had to go to the bathroom, but then Dounia became angry and restless and slapped at Madame's abdomen, so Madame sent Lema and Abudi and Nisrine and me with her to pee.

"Stay in there," Madame said, and she closed the door on us. Nisrine knocked to get out. She wouldn't open it. Nisrine had been locked in once before, and she had kept repeating for the last two days, *Never again*. But, here she was. She threw herself against the door. Adel was supposed to help us. Madame didn't open.

We huddled in the muggy leftovers smell of the bathroom, while Dounia sat to pee in the middle of us. Outside, we could hear boots and Madame praying. "Aya, aya," Madame prayed, her voice rising.

Dounia sat peeing.

Over her noise, the rest of us stood ears to the door, listening.

Dounia reached for the orange hose beside the toilet to wash her pee when she was done, then she used a sheet from the dirty laundry pile to dry.

Dounia asked, "Bea, you know him up there?" She pointed to the bathroom ceiling.

Lema said, "Hush, Dounia."

"You mean the neighbors?"

"No. In the sky."

"You mean God?"

Lema said, "*Haram*, don't say it in the bathroom. It's dirty."

Outside, the front door opened and closed. There were more boots and voices. Madame was still praying.

"He was supposed to come," Nisrine repeated, "he was supposed to come."

We had been trying for so long to think up plans, Nisrine and I. For her to grow her heart, so she could stay. For her to leave. For me to grow my heart. To help Baba, to fix things, and they had all centered on Adel. He had been the middle of all of them; our hopes had curled around him like soft petals around the yellow center of a flower. Nisrine loved many people, she fit them all in her heart, but Adel had been her only hope, here. He had been the one who would help us.

Slowly, her knees gave way and she sank, small and pink in her pajamas, to the damp tile floor. The children and I crowded around and breathed on her like trees.

We sat together and listened to the sounds of Baba being taken.

After a little while, Abudi had to pee, so because he was older and a boy, Lema and Dounia and I turned our backs on him. Nisrine's head was already bent. Then, when Abudi was done, I had to pee, so the children and Nisrine all turned their backs for me, and I crouched over the toilet, moisture on my eyelids, feeling the sloppy waste smell in my pores. Halfway through, Dounia became curious. She wanted to look, she wouldn't turn away, so Lema grabbed Dounia and forced her head to her stomach so I, too, could pee in privacy, my nose at Dounia's back, my elbow beside Abudi, my eyes on the tips of hair that had escaped from Nisrine's and Lema's white veils.

WHEN MADAME LET US OUT, the apartment was quiet and empty.

Dounia asked, "Where's Baba?"

"He went with the police." Madame was filling water bottles for the night in the kitchen. Nisrine and I stood palely beside her, not helping.

I asked, "What do we do now?"

"We wait."

"Aren't you going to call someone?"

"Our phones are watched. He'll come back if he's not taken."

But I wanted to call someone, anyone. It was not yet dinnertime, and I was full of bathroom smell and police and we must do something, I must call someone.

In the morning, it had snowed. In the afternoon, police had come, and in the space of that time we had lost Baba.

The phone rang. Madame picked it up. "We're fine. Yes, everything's fine. Can you believe the snow?" She said it over and over again, into the phone. "Can you believe the snow?"

When she hung up, I said, "I could call my embassy, to see what they say."

"The embassy only helps Americans."

"Maybe not. Maybe they help everyone."

Madame looked at me. "Our phones are watched."

Here, it was always if you loved them, then.

In America, I relied on the government when I had a need. In natural disaster or unemployment, our government was supposed to have programs to bail us out. But here, there was no low-interest loan from the bank, no government aid, so people relied on their families. Perhaps that was why every day we told the same stories, about family ties and duty, and if you loved them, then you would call. If you loved them, then you would help. If you loved them, then you would stay with them for a very long time and never leave, and you would listen, and you would tell, you would tell them they're kind to you, you would tell them you loved them, and they would comfort you when you were sad, they would comfort you if you cried, which could be often because you were American, and a woman.

Madame washed parsley to eat with cheese. She gave me a bunch, and I sat at the table, to sort the yellow from the green.

I had come here to cry for an astonishing text.

Madame said, "What's the matter, Bea?"

"Nothing." I was sorting parsley.

Madame said, "Don't cry on it. It's unsanitary. Here, give those to me." She took the stems from me and began to sort them herself.

If you loved them, then you would not ask questions about Baba's life before jail, his first family, or Nisrine's Indonesian family, because you did not care about past lives, this was your life now, this was important. You may fight, but only inside. You would always take their side, and you would not talk about them to tutors or police, or anyone outside the house. They were your life now, talking about them to others would only hurt yourself.

I wiped my eyes.

After a while, Madame sighed and patted my cheek. "I think having Hassan in the house depresses me. I used to have cheeks just like yours before I was married, Bea. I had full cheeks, just like yours."

Nisrine did not try to call like I did, she knew this was useless. She sat, looking pale and thoughtful.

"Why didn't he come?" she asked. "I thought we understood each other. I thought, when he came to me across the sky, that he was something greater than myself." Together, they had been making a new language.

She shook her head.

In the evening, we got a call from Moni confirming that Baba would spend the night in jail. When she got off the phone, Madame searched her purse for money. She searched her underwear drawer, and all Baba's shoes and his jeans and even his dirty shirt pockets and between the covers of his books. Then, she came to me.

"How much do you have?"

"How much do you want?"

"Well, we need to eat."

I handed her my purse and she dumped all of it onto the table. Then we went through my pants pockets and my underwear drawer, and I gave her the money we found.

That night, Nisrine gathered up all the poems Adel had written, and the children and I watched her tear them, one by one, and release them over the balcony, where the wind took them.

"I miss him, Bea."

I felt a pain in my heart for the poems. They danced before our window like snow.

"Look how light they are. I want to be light like that." She had wanted to fly off like them.

"Words," Nisrine said, "only words."

IT WAS THE NIGHT my mother was supposed to call.

Madame said, "Don't tell her about what happened today, just say everything's fine."

"Everything's fine?"

"You can't talk about it, Baba's in jail. If you talk, Baba might get in more trouble. You wouldn't want to put him in more trouble."

"No."

"Just say you're well, and we send kisses. Tell your mother I send kisses."

My cell phone rang. It was my mother.

"How are things there, Bea? Are you still thinking of coming home? I hear on the TV there's been unrest."

"Everything's fine."

Madame blew kisses at the phone.

"Madame here kisses you."

My mother was flattered. She made kissing sounds. "Here's for you and Madame." She made more kissing sounds. "Is Dounia there? Does she send kisses?"

Dounia was twirling around like she'd been doing since the morning, being a snowflake.

"She's here. She sends kisses."

"Well, kiss her for me, then, too."

. . .

With Baba gone, there was a bed for each of us, and we each had our new place to sleep. I no longer slept with Lema; Lema slept in Madame's bed, because Madame was not sleeping, she was on Baba's sofa in the living room, watching TV. All night she sat with the TV tuned to the religious stations, a bottle of water between her clean feet. When I woke for the bathroom, she turned off the TV very quickly, and pretended to fall asleep.

WAITING

THIS IS WHAT HAPPENS when someone goes missing: your body shrinks, and the missing grows.

When my parents divorced, I got a stomachache that lasted and lasted, and wouldn't go away, and for a little while it felt like I became my stomach; the rest of me shriveled, and all I could think about was my little pain.

The next morning after Baba was taken, there was a thin line that ran between Madame and Nisrine and me, and as we did the housework, or played with the children, I could feel them where they were, thinking about Baba, and I could feel me where I was, thinking about Baba, and it was as if all of us, Madame and Nisrine and the children and me, were one big brain that thought, Baba. We had not forgotten our differences, but for the moment, they were put aside, and we moved about the house like birds together, migrating from room to room. When someone was hungry, we ate. When someone was tired, we rested.

We carried our waiting. Like Nisrine's gas, it clung to my sweater drawer and Arabic books, and our bras and pajama pants and underwear, which was all we wore around the house now because there was no need for shirts, when Abudi was still young and Baba was gone. His absence granted us this small freedom.

Free women, we waited, and as we waited, the missing grew. I searched again and again for people to call on my cell phone. I looked for Adel on the roof of the station.

By afternoon we became so bored waiting that even little things and sad things, like death, became scandalous. The widow who didn't cry when her husband died. Our neighbor's daughter, who beat her chest and threw her veil. We laughed, sighed, shook our heads.

Madame made long lists of the suitors who came to engage her before Baba, and she pinched Dounia's toes for each one:

Simsim who lived in Maisaat. His shoe size was very large.

An old man who owned twelve buildings, but he was so ugly she couldn't look at him. He sat in front of her high school every day, reading the Quran.

Her cousin, but she didn't like him, so she told him, Put one of your houses in my name. Of course, he wouldn't. She knew he wouldn't, that was why she said it. How else do you refuse your cousin?

One whose mother refused Madame, but he wouldn't have anyone else, so he didn't marry for two years.

One who had an old wife already and just wanted children.

Oh, the tedium! Like dust, it climbed the walls, sat in the hall, in the locked door we kept waiting for Baba to open. Waiting, we lost our sense of connection. We did chores to pass the time. To keep up appearances, we washed Baba's pants and hung them on the balcony to dry, as if he still needed them.

Small people, small battles.

Madame said, "I told you it would be warmer today," and in her voice was satisfaction. "You want me to put your sweater inside for you, Bea?"

"No, I can do it."

It was the time I usually met with Imad.

Madame looked at the kitchen clock. "No lesson today?"

"No."

"Good, stay here with us. I'll take you to the National Library."

Madame told all of us to dress, even Nisrine. With all that had happened, we could not leave her behind in the house. There was a flurry not to be the last one ready. We got down the children's good shoes from their boxes in the closet, and looked for gifts to give the librarian. Madame searched for the perfume I once gave her.

"You said the librarian was a woman, Bea?"

There were six of us ready at the door, which was the number Madame's family had been before they gained me, and we were all in our outdoor skirts and outdoor jeans, even Nisrine. For this event, she had taken off her pajamas. We crowded into the elevator, talking and giggling, and pushed the buttons over and over. We hadn't gone on an outing like this before, it was an adventure.

On the way down, we talked about car bombs. Madame said, "Who'll start Baba's car for us?"

Abudi was a big boy, almost ten. He volunteered.

Madame wouldn't let him. "You're too short," she told him. "You have to be taller than the dashboard."

We walked out of the elevator, joking about short Abudi, so Abudi hit Dounia in the chest. He ran back inside and wouldn't come out until Madame went to go get him. While we waited, the rest of us jumped over small puddles the sun made on melted snow. It had gathered under the bushes and beneath the swing set. Dounia jumped in a puddle and splashed Nisrine.

"Dounia!"

The sun shone yellow like summer. She slipped off her coat.

Madame came back with Abudi, and we returned to who was driving.

Not Lema, she wasn't old enough.

Not Madame, Baba never taught her.

Not Nisrine, not me—

"Why not?" Madame asked. "You drive in America, don't you, Bea?"

For a moment, I thought about car bombs. Then, I thought of the library.

"OK." I held out my hand for the keys.

. . .

We approached the car cautiously. At the curb, Madame told the children to stay back. She wanted me to start the engine alone, in case there really was a bomb inside, she didn't want multiple casualties. "One's enough!" she joked, toes over the curb, brightly.

I didn't think it was very funny.

I walked over to the car. While I unlocked the door, the children shouted encouragements.

"Don't worry, Bea, Americans are bombproof!"

"Don't worry, Bea. Matt *mat*. You can join your tutor, he's already dead, haha!"

I sat down and put the key in. "Here I go," I said.

At the last minute, Dounia wriggled away from Nisrine, who had been holding her, and ran toward me as I started the ignition—"Dounia!" But it didn't matter, because then Dounia and I were still alive, and the car was running. I drove down the block with the children trailing behind me, joking, no longer worried about bombs.

We began our outing. I was driving, with Madame and Abudi in the front seat, and Dounia and Lema and Nisrine in the back where the sun came down strong, so Lema complained about her complexion. She hid under Dounia's skirt to stop the sun. We rolled down all the windows and hung our arms out. Dounia sang songs in Arabic while the rest of us clapped along.

And, as I gripped the wheel, my fingers tense with excitement,

I noticed a similar feeling in Nisrine. She looked around at a city she had seen only from above: the dirty sidewalks, the glittery pavement, the wavy head-sized top of a garden bush. I watched her roll down her window and reach out to those now life-size objects, trying to brush the sides of them as we passed. This city was teeming with life and color: purse yellow of the chamomile flowers, deep red of the store awnings, blue of a religious woman's coat. She thrust her head out, opened her arms wide, pushed back her veil to greet it.

"Hello, beautiful!" she called. Across the sky, white clouds moved like wings.

In Arabic, the word for freedom is *hurriya*. I remember first learning this word as a beginning student, and memorizing it by its nearness to the English word "hurray."

The joy it brought me.

I had also never seen our city like this. Watching Nisrine, I gained new eyes. We passed by lemon trees, a pale fountain. I had never sat in the front seat of a car here; as we drove, the wind lifted our hair to the beat of Dounia's singing. We made our way down the street, hands out the window, and were not stopped by any policemen.

Nisrine said, "I want always to feel this," about the wind.

The National Library was gray and foreboding in the sun. Lema, who had never been, took one look and said, "Bea, are you sure this is where you want to go?"

We traipsed in quietly. At the door, Madame told us to wait while she went up to the desk. She put the perfume we had brought in the front pocket of her purse, ready to give, then started slowly forward.

The rest of us held our breath. When Dounia coughed, Lema put her hand over her mouth. We watched Madame approach the librarian, whose head was bent over a book.

"Excuse me," Madame said.

The librarian didn't look up.

"Excuse me," Madame said again, reaching for the perfume, but she didn't need it, because a strange thing happened: as the librarian lifted her head, Madame started beaming. "Hunadi!" she exclaimed, and to my surprise, the librarian didn't tell Madame to lower her voice. She came around the front of the desk and the two women kissed on both cheeks. She asked about Madame's family, her mother and children.

After a few minutes, Madame came back to us, smiling.

"Come on, Bea. You're going to see the astonishing text."

I couldn't believe it.

"That's Hunadi. Why didn't you tell me she was the librarian? I know her from grade school. Her sister and I were best friends."

The librarian came over, too. "Who's going?" she asked.

"Bea is."

She looked at Madame and Nisrine, the other adults. "Do you want to go with her?" They each paused. Nisrine said, "I'll stay with the children," but Nisrine had taught me all I knew about love, and in these last few days, she and Madame and I had been doing everything together, our usual roles in the family had changed. I took her hand. "Come with me."

Madame said she would come, too, so the librarian got out three pairs of cotton gloves for us to put on, told the children to stay at the door where they couldn't reach to touch anything, and Nisrine and Madame and I followed her past the cage where scholars sat, past the empty shelves, through a small door, to a room full of books.

So, this was where they kept them! I looked around me. Books sat everywhere, in piles three high on the shelving, on top of vaults for old relics. I reached out to touch one; its corner came away like dust in my gloved hand. Layers and layers of books. Histories and maps and biographies; a map of the city when our apartment was a lemon grove; a map of the town where Madame grew up, when it was a grazing ground for goats. There were hundreds of books, and they seemed without order or plan, as if anyone who walked in would be equally happy with any of them, and standing there breathing in their worn-out smell, I thought anyone would be. I hadn't seen so many books since I arrived. Here was the autobiography of the president. Here was Aramaic, a biblical language.

Nisrine's eyes were bright. She looked around, taking in the titles the same way she had taken in the colors of this city's buildings.

"Bea, so this is why you like this place!"

The librarian told us to wait. She went into yet another, smaller room and came out a moment later, holding a thin leather case, which she cleared a space for on one of the dusty tables.

"Go ahead," she said.

Neither Madame nor Nisrine nor I moved.

"Go on, don't you want your text?" She undid the casing, shook it once, and five perfect pages like light slid out.

In the great stories of Arabic writing, scholars often recount the moment they see a truly astonishing text. It changes them. Forever afterwards, they live with the memory.

Madame and Nisrine and I approached our text carefully. The writing was beautiful but simple, spaced delicately over the center of the page. Painted vines ran along the sides, curving lightly in toward one perfect blue flower.

Madame said, "That's the flower of the desert. It blooms only once every hundred years."

Nisrine put out a finger to touch it. Adel had once called her this flower.

"It's lovely," she said, and I remembered the last time she said this, about Adel's first poem, leaning, a dishrag in one hand, against the counter. That had been the first text we'd shared.

What is the beauty of experience, if not felt with those close to you? I had once received a poem, and ran with it to Nisrine, and there may have been moments afterwards when I regretted it, when I saw how that poem led to love for her, and for me—what? But, I never regretted the actual sharing; two heads bent over the same bright pages, two hearts simultaneous in anticipation, holding the same long breath. I always cherished that memory. I still do.

And even the writer, when she writes, isn't it, too, to share?

. . .

We began to read. Silently at first, side by side, faces squeezed close so we could see. I traced the lines with my finger, the perfect vines, the tightly spun letters. After a moment, I heard a low hum in Madame's throat; it grew, until she began to recite in a low, sing-song voice, the way Baba used to pray, or recite the Quran. So, I stopped tracing the words, Nisrine stopped mouthing them, and instead, we followed along while Madame sang to us, an ancient love story.

The first page of the text was for Qais; we saw him in the letters, the light touch of gold in his breath and his poems; the love he gave Leila from afar, arms open, the edge of the page an unbearable distance between them, yearning like the layers of Leila's tent. Their love was sweet, it filled them with happiness; each in their separate world, it took only a glimpse, like the flash of a blue flower, to fill the rest of their hours with joy.

And as I began to read I, too, felt joy; I saw each word and met it, joyfully, with understanding.

But as we read on, sadness crept in. There was trouble; just like that, their love had changed. Glimpses were no longer enough for them—what was a glimpse of Leila, when she remained far away from him, when her eyes were so sad? The page became empty, the letters far apart, and we knew this marked Leila's leaving. All around were whispers of Qais's longing, the *hamza* a deep hole; the line's end a finality, like banishment.

We read on, now of Qais's wanderings. He was no longer called Qais, only Crazy for Leila. But though Leila was gone, we still felt her in the text; her essence was everywhere in the elegance of the letters, like a young woman's straight back. The fear in Qais, heavy as a policeman's boots.

And what I saw was how place didn't matter, and at first, this uplifted me. Leila was gone, but her essence remained, even in the word "leaving," or "banished," the small *e* like the sweet curve of her chin. Poor Qais, he would never forget her, she was his garden aflame, all red henna and raw wandering. Without her, he was only two sand-sore eyes, and I almost cried for this, but I didn't. I thought, Love is everywhere, it follows you, and at first this seemed a joyous thing, how we are able to love, even after the lover has left us, how memory can live on.

But, even as I felt joy, the words began to fall in on themselves, and I saw how painful love could be. Leila was everywhere, and Qais missed her after she left. And I saw, too, how missing does not stay in one place, but spreads out like snow; how it dusts everything, and changes the landscape. How it is what you carry with you, what you see and breathe, and so Qais no longer talked of Leila to his friends, or the shepherd, but she was everywhere with him, in his language, in the curve of the painted page, and of course, I saw this then, a breath of it, because of missing Baba. And I see it now, am destined always to see it, because of Nisrine.

Madame sang, her voice low and watery. Love blended with Qais's daily tasks, until it became his daily task, until there was no difference between the love and the missing and the daily task of minding a shepherd's sheep. Love is something you learn to live with, forever. It does not stop after death; it does not stop when someone leaves; it did not, has not, for me.

Nisrine turned to me. There were tears on her cheeks. "It's an impossible situation, Bea. Qais loved, but his loving couldn't help her."

There were tears in Madame's eyes, too.

"Don't cry, Bea."

"Don't cry, Nisrine."

"Don't cry, Mama."

I had come to cry for an astonishing text. But, as I leaned against Madame and Nisrine, feeling their tears in my hair, feeling mine on Nisrine's shoulder, I knew a truth about us three: we were not crying for the text, the way I had thought I would when I came here. I saw the words, and I saw Leila in the words, and then they blurred until I no longer saw their beauty, but it didn't matter. We were not crying for words, but because men whom we loved had gone, and they loomed large, and we missed them. And I have cried since, too, but never for a text; rather, because after Baba, Nisrine also left, and I know that even if I try my whole life, no amount of words will fill the hole that her leaving made.

So far, I have found this to be true. And yet, like the shepherd and like Qais, I have kept trying.

We read on.

The third page was the shepherd's. He came to Qais with thick frizzed hair and a smooth stick, and suddenly the letters of the text grew quiet. They contemplated the long silences of life in the desert. They contemplated the ease with which Qais talked and the shepherd listened. And as the words went on, drawing us forward with Madame's voice, the love story began to seem like a love story of three. I saw how the shepherd loved both Qais and Leila, and watched over them, and over Qais's poems, and I thought, Qais and Leila's romance ended, but their love did not, and neither did the shepherd's. And, I have since thought of the shepherd, how he loved, and watched both lovers, and I have come to see that this is the problem of the shepherd: how to stay behind and care for love when the lovers don't remain?

I have had to find my own way in this.

We read on. We three were together now, linked over the text, our hands and chests and eyes mingling.

What else did I notice? That it didn't use the words I expected. I had learned so many words in Arabic that meant love, and yet this text showed its love not through those words, but with simple ones, small actions—the way the shepherd held his staff when he listened to Qais. The way Qais took Leila's name.

I thought back to how I was called Baba.

I thought back to the word Madame liked about Baba that I didn't understand.

I thought back to all the moments without words that I held in my heart, and I thought, Of course. Why did I study words that meant love? Love is not in what is said, but what is done, what is felt and experienced, it is the intimacy of silent moments, of small meanings.

In the story, the shepherd knew this. He stayed beside Qais, and loved him, and loved Leila, but eventually, Leila left and Qais went crazy, and both were lost. I had first known the shepherd as the keeper of Qais's poems, and I had been drawn to him for this image, but now, I saw this was not the most important part of him. Rather, he was a man who felt deeply; sometimes, the only way to express deep feeling is through a story.

And so it is that I learned the astonishing text was not just a text of love, but also loss. Or, if it is of love, then it is only because the line is so fine between loss and love; because we almost never feel loss without first feeling love, and perhaps the opposite is also true.

I had been looking all along for a language of love, and I finally found that what drove the shepherd to write, what would drive me, too, was loss. Loss moved his beautiful words, and this was not a choice. He wrote, because he had nothing else left to do.

And, years later, I would sit in a room in a warm house, winter out my window, a box of poems and letters laid before me, and think, Since I left Madame's, since that day with the text, I have tried to run away from words, but in the end, for me, too, there is nothing else left. By this point, I knew that words were not the same as experience; that love is something you feel, not something you read. But, having felt love at Madame's and lost it, and having seen the world of those I loved come undone around me, I turned back to words. Imperfect though they are, they are still something.

And, perhaps in turning back, I can thank the shepherd. (And Adel, who grew tired of his poems, so sent them to me.) I read through the text that day feeling both joy and sorrow. Joy at the power of memory, sorrow at how all three of these—Qais, and the shepherd, and Leila—were powerless against what they felt.

Toward the end the shepherd began to give up, and in my heart, I, too, felt myself release, wallow in his hopelessness, think we are all done for, powerless against what we feel. But then, at the very bottom of the last page—a signature.

I turned to Madame. "What's that?"

She wiped her eyes. "It's the sign of the shepherd."

I had thought Qais was the poet. "The shepherd wrote this?"

"Yes."

So, he hadn't given up, he had kept trying. From loss had sprung the most beautiful words.

While I wrestled and keened before all this, Nisrine, who knew loss and love, whose family was far away, who had just lost a deep love, a constant ache in her heart, also learned her own quiet lesson.

She leaned over to me, her voice watery. "Qais loved Leila, and yet he couldn't help her."

I paused. This lesson was hers, not mine.

"Love does not always mean help. Sometimes, you have to be like the bird and fly yourself. Remember the bird in my story, Bea? How, all by herself, she flew away?"

The bird, who had followed her heart, who was neither Qais nor Leila, and so had learned to live on her own.

In the car on the way home, Madame and Nisrine and I were silent. The children felt our fragile mood.

Nisrine squinted at street signs, as if she were memorizing them.

We rode the elevator in silence, but it was a silence we entered together, and we were kind to one another; we took arms, held the door, helped with shoes.

In the kitchen, Madame told Lema and Nisrine and me to fold the laundry, while she put milk on to boil. Abudi came in as we were folding and took a shirt to put under his shirt, beside his belly.

"Look, I'm pregnant!"

"What did your mother-in-law say?"

"I left her celebrating. She was throwing rice off the balcony."

The phone rang. Madame answered it. She leaned against the stove, listening, then she hung up and came over to where Nisrine and Lema and I were, to help us fold.

"That was Moni," Madame said. "Hassan's been charged, they know who informed on him, it was that tutor. He said Baba and his friends were at the Journalists' Club. You didn't tell your tutor Baba was at the Journalists' Club, did you, Bea?"

For a moment, I didn't say anything. Like Nisrine with the gas a long time ago, I wanted to blame Abudi. I had been so careful not to tell about Baba's document. But, I remembered us, locked in.

What about the father?

He's at the Journalists' Club.

Where the document was. The place police knew was for resisters. Where the resisters had signed.

Abudi knew better. Abudi didn't talk to strange men.

. . .

All day, I had been learning lessons about words, and perhaps here was my last one: that more important than all the words in Arabic is the ability to keep silent, to know when not to speak.

Lema was folding laundry. She'd made a neat pile of our shirts on the kitchen table, and another neat pile for our underwear. She took my shirt and balled it in her fist, to crumple it. She looked at Madame.

"She just stuffs them in her drawer, anyway. It's our work, and she messes it up."

The milk boiled.

Nisrine came over to me. She said, "It's OK, Bea. It was a slip, you didn't mean it."

Madame got up to turn off the gas. She spread dried yogurt and jelly on bread for the children, then handed Nisrine and me each a bowl with what was left.

"No, thank you, Mama, I'm not hungry."

"Finish it, Bea, we've all had our share."

I was the reason Baba was in jail and so I was deeply in debt. I didn't know how to make it right, so I pretended family debts were like money debts, with a finite number, and I looked for little forms of payment, to make it up in small, jelly-bowl-size increments.

"You finish it, Mama. I'm not hungry."

Madame passed the bowl to Abudi, and my debt kept looming.

Lema said, "Go home, Bea. You must be tired of us."

"Yes, Bea, go home."

At Madame's, we were wary with strangers, so we were careless with one another instead. When Madame was angry, she hit Dounia. When I was upset, I closed the bathroom door and didn't care that others needed it. Abudi was the only boy. He ordered his sisters to get him his shoes and Nisrine to make him his snacks. He lay in waiting to kick them, and when Madame found out she didn't beat him. This was Abudi's privilege, kicking and not being beaten.

I also had a privilege: mine was carelessness with information. Because I was foreign and American, I met strangers in the street and talked openly to tutors and police, and I wasn't taken.

But, Baba was taken.

He would have gone to jail at some point, no matter what, he had signed a document. But, because of me and my tutor, he had gone now.

Of course, I wanted to make it up, to undo what I spoke, I saw how fluency isn't vocabulary—

Madame stopped me. There was more.

"Moni says the blond one is no longer police. There's a rumor that his father beat him, because he found out about a love affair. They took away his uniform."

And now we all looked at Nisrine, who had relinquished Adel, whom we had watched tear up his poems one by one.

She stood beside me, her arm in my arm. I felt her stiffen.

So, this was why he had not come for her, because they had been found out. In the end, it was not Madame who we needed to hide their love from, but his father who had beat him. We could see the pain of this information.

And, I know now how it all connected:

A simple sentence, *He's at the Journalists' Club.*

A simple confession, to save a tutoring business.

A simple report, in the wrong blond man's hands: Adel had been reading Imad's confession; it had been on his desk, he had seen the note about Baba, and he had been planning to help us, when his father came in. His father, who was already angry at his son for loving the wrong woman.

If he had not loved that woman; if she had not loved him back; if I had not loved them both, would the rest have happened?

Qais wrote poems for Leila, and when he lost her, he went crazy. I am sure afterwards, regrets ran through his head: If he hadn't sent Leila poems, then. If he had worked harder and kept more sheep, then. If he had been kinder to her father, then. If he hadn't stood before her tent so obviously, what might have turned out differently?

In Arabic, like in most languages, these thoughts are called the subjunctive, and they are formed by combining the past and future tense. And I am sure the same thoughts that occurred to Qais so long ago also occurred to Madame and Nisrine in that moment, like they occurred to me.

If we had not—

If I had not—

If our hearts were not what they were.

Nisrine did not like the subjunctive.

Adel had once said, *If I could touch you—*

And she'd stopped him, *When you touch me.*

If you love me—

Hush, I do.

All this time, Nisrine had waited in a house where she loved, but also hurt; where she cared, but did not always feel wanted; a house that had closed in around her, that she could not seem to escape.

From the astonishing text, she had taken this lesson: that missing is everywhere, and grows large. That love cannot always help; that sometimes we must simply take hold ourselves; that it is better not to be Qais and Leila, but rather to be like the bird in her own story who flew when she needed, and followed her own heart.

From Madame, she had learned that a man she loved lay hurt, maybe in need of her, beaten for her love. She must have felt the responsibility of this, too.

And here, because I don't want to tell what happens next,

because I want so badly in this story, like in life, to delay the moment—I will tell you instead, this: that love is a wide-open space. That it can be friendship and passion and leaving and unrequited all at once. That I have loved and kissed many times in my life, but no love has changed me like Nisrine.

It was too much. Earlier, she had said, *It's an impossible situation.*

I stood still that day, and listened to my part in Madame's information.

Nisrine didn't, she moved.

She squeezed my hand, then ran to the front door. "Adel!" she cried. It was locked. Madame tried to grab her, but she slipped away; her veil caught for a moment, then unraveled and her hair fell out. She made for the balcony, and I don't know if she meant to call to Adel again, or to climb hand over hand on a rope like he had, or if she only wanted to stay a moment outside, to feel cool air on her face—I will never know, I can only guess.

The balcony was wet with melted snow, and the rail jiggled.

"Nisrine," I called, wanting to help, to share in this moment. She didn't look back.

She went out with her arms open, slipped, knocked against the rail, which gave—loss stretched out before me.

She fell, her veil a white wing behind her, five floors down to the garden below.

AFTERWARDS, I remember very little. I seemed to float. Men came and went in formal uniforms. Madame took care of them. Eventually, she called Moni, who came to get me in her car and take me to my agency, where they called my mother to send a plane ticket for me, and just like that—even in that state, I felt the injustice of this—I flew home.

AMERICA

ALL THIS HAPPENED A LONG TIME AGO, yet it is still vivid. Memory comes when you least expect it, jogged by simple things—the way my older mother holds a knife, just as Madame used to; translucent purple, the color of parsley in iodine; the sound and shape of so many words that remind me of Nisrine.

This is the problem with missing: it doesn't stay in one place, but spreads out and changes the landscape.

Memory takes the smallest detail, and turns it luminous, so you miss even the mundane parts of a person, the ones you didn't know you would.

Nisrine had a knowing air about her, sometimes. Like Madame, she used little things—housework—against me, and because she wouldn't tell me why, she left me with no way to make it up.

She knew more about love than me, she'd had more experience, and she let me know this, not by saying it, but by her silences, her *tsk tsk* gestures, like I sometimes let her know I'd had more opportunity for Arabic classes; we didn't want to be that way with each other, we just were. It was part of what made us, us.

And yet, Nisrine had the ability to end any fight she wanted, this is true, I'm not exaggerating—she was simply that funny, I remember the rub like warm coats on our stomachs, falling over each other, laughing—and she was that kind, and I loved her that much.

And, how do you come back from that love, or, once lost, the missing? Once changed, how do you return to a previous, pristine world? In the Quran, like the Bible, the changed world is earth, the place the first lovers went after they were banished from Eden, and there, they found sorrow and pain. They were taken aback, cried out, This is not what we expected! But of course, this is the curse of knowledge: to see all earth's imperfections, always.

And, isn't there some truth to this story, even now? That the act of knowing is really just the confrontation of sorrow; the gathering of our forces, and finding a way forward, toward love, still? Isn't that, anyway, what we hope?

And, what if the love that we found was not meant to be shared just between two people, but by many; a fiery, starry substance that grows when it's kindled, so that the more you love and are beloved, the more light?

What if we really can hold all the hearts we ever wanted, and when we die, we are able to flit among them—the person who dies is able to visit any country where there's someone who loved her, and so for Nisrine, whose loves spanned continents and ages, then there is infinite travel, infinite coming and going, an infinite amount of light. What if death were not death, but adventure? Would I miss her, then, this much?

I RETURNED TO AMERICA EARLY, still in loose pants and long shirts out of respect, and swaying like a lost leaf under this uniform. My mother took one look at me and put me to bed, and that is where I stayed for much of the summer. Nisrine stayed with me. I closed my eyes and felt I was in a foreign country; my body had flown, but my mind could not.

Fall came, and my mother, with her sturdy Midwestern sense, sent me back to university. There, I felt very little—I didn't want to feel. Months passed like that, until I finally learned again to respond to my classmates in discussion and lose myself in books. I did this mostly out of instinct, because I was alive, and it is our job, when we are alive, to try to keep living. Eventually, instinct became habit, and from habit, I learned again to be myself, though always a little different, like the sound of your voice in a new language, which is always a little high or low.

Now, when I find it hard to wake up, I remember Nisrine, and I try to set my teeth like she did, stare out the window, try to make myself as light as possible, like swimming through slow water. I think, If I am here, then I will float; if I am destined always to carry this place, these people with me, then at least let me carry them forward. And I have. I am studying for an advanced degree, to be a scholar, something Nisrine always predicted for me. I search for meaning in deep words. In this way, I keep her close.

LIKE I SAID, I don't remember the end of Nisrine's death. That time has flown.

I do know that the following week, Madame learned Nisrine's whole name and her family's name from the Indonesian embassy, and while I sat on a plane barreling across the ocean, Madame gathered up the money she owed Nisrine and wired it, minus the fee, to her family. She did this on her own, without Baba or me to help her. It was very hard for Madame to go out; every time she did, she had to take all the children with her, and none of them could drive, so they rode the bus, which was dirty.

She says that Nisrine's family was gracious. A sister thanked her in Arabic. They had already learned of Nisrine's death from her embassy, who had shown up almost at the same time as the doctors, and taken over. In life, Nisrine had been Madame's maid, but in death she became again, foremost, a citizen. The embassy gathered her up and sent her, along with a few belongings, home. There, finally, her family met her, their mother, their wife, their daughter, their sister, and mourned.

ON THE PHONE, Madame is always the same. She gives her love to my mother, and I give my love to all her children, who are grown now, but in the beginning lined up one by one so she could put the receiver to their ears, one by one, to hear that I missed them.

She has never reproached me for my part in Baba's jail, or Nisrine's death. Perhaps she hears in my voice already the way these two faces give me sleepless nights, unspun days. Or, perhaps she is simply too busy; she's raised three children alone.

Over the years, Madame and I have learned again to laugh and tease. I have heard all about Lema's suitors, who began to come the year after I left, though Madame wouldn't let her marry until she turned eighteen. They sat in the parlor with Madame and Abudi while Lema served the tea. One of them was much older than Lema, twice her age, so she called him Uncle by mistake, but he still liked her. It became a joke between them, and now they have a son. Madame says motherhood has been good to Lema, she has grown very pretty. "What about you, Bea?" she asks. "Are you next?"

And I laugh to hide my discomfort. In Madame's country, I am very old already not to have a husband and child. Both of us know this.

Madame says, "I hope it's not anything you saw here, which discourages you," and I tell her it's not. Her house, I tell her, is where I learned about love. Having learned this, it's hard to settle for anything else.

So, Madame doesn't ask about husbands, and though I want to, I don't ask about Baba, because on the phone, we still don't mention husbands by name. Instead I wait, and trust that if there was news, if Baba was released, or if Madame was allowed to see him, then she would tell me. Two years after I left he was freed briefly, but he began his activities again and was rearrested.

The document he signed is now famous. A very brave declaration, it was one of the documents that gave his fellow countrymen the courage to call for a new government. They are still calling for this.

As I write, Madame's country is at war, like much of the Middle East.

For the first year of the war, Madame stayed. When she and I talked on the phone, we each wanted to know what the other knew. She thought because I was American, I must have special information. I thought because she was there, she must have special information, but Madame stayed inside, and in America I stayed inside, and we both watched the same news.

In the second year of the war, it became difficult. There were shortages and price hikes. Abudi, who was sixteen, no longer a boy, reported men in long lines before bread ovens. Sometimes, he would go out in the morning for food and not get home until evening. Madame no longer had to skim cream off the top of the milk for Dounia's diet, the milk just came watery. There was no money. The children went out and wandered the old markets, but the markets were empty. Bombs fell where the family could feel them, and Abudi agitated to fight. He no longer went to school, he searched out soldiers in the streets and so, though Baba was still in jail, Madame decided they must leave. She lives now with Baba's sister and waits, like I do, for news of him. There is a note for him on the kitchen table, where Nisrine's notes and my notes used to sit. It's written on small lined paper in Madame's neat hand: *Hassan, leave the house. Be sensible, come for us.* It stays there, hoping like we do, waiting for Baba's release.

THERE IS A VERSION of "Qais and Leila" in Farsi that I have found many American students know. In this version, the lovers never kiss, but they meet again in heaven, where they don't part, even for a moment; when one is hungry, they are both hungry, when one is tired, they both sleep, and so in the end, there is a merging and a reckoning, and this justice lasts for eternity.

How to trust that justice will be done?

There was an inquiry into Nisrine's death, but Madame's country has poor building codes, and so no one was found to blame. Still, many people felt bad. When she talked to Nisrine's sister, all Madame could say, over and over, was how sorry she was. Despite their sadness, the family continued to be gracious.

"What will you tell her child?" Madame asked.

On the phone, there was a pause. Then, the sister answered, "We will tell him that his mother is like any heroine."

The word, which means a maid who travels, and a house that moves, and the protagonist of an adventure.

"We will tell him she's on a long journey."

. . .

Now, Nisrine's son is almost twelve. I have written letters to him, and his aunt has helped him to write back. I imagine him, growing strong and firm like she was. I imagine the happiest life for him; patience like his grandfather's to buy flowers beside burnt buildings; strength like his mother's to travel to far-off places, to give up control of her child and her passport, to love languages, even those forced upon her, to love Dounia and Adel, to love me, to love home.

I imagine her son, waiting patiently for his heroine-mother. Of course, he is older now. He knows that hers was a journey from which one can't return. If his family is religious, then they've tried to comfort him: *You'll see her in the next life.*

Even so, I imagine a small part of him still waits for her in this one. He knows she is gone, but can he ever truly stop hoping? If he can't, if he does wait, does hope, does watch for the end of a journey, birds like sooty fingerprints at the edge of the horizon—then, this is something he and I share.

Regardless, I imagine the happiest life for him. Nisrine believed in a god and a powerful fate. He won't forsake her child.

We both remember the story of the woman who once flew to the rainbow: if she can make it there, she can make it back.

THE SHEPHERD LOVED, and he lost, and out of his loss came words, because he had nothing else to give.

I have memory, and it follows me, but we don't choose our memories, only how we carry them, and so in an effort to carry differently, I write.

I never talked to Imad again; I suppose I am not as good at forgiving as Madame is. But, I do keep in touch with Adel. He called me soon after he recovered. Through the phone, I heard the same rough edge of guilt and sadness that I also felt, and though I worried for him, it comforted me. We cannot lessen each other's missing, but together we stave off its loneliness.

Like me, Adel has never married. In the aftermath of Nisrine, he wandered, lost. A policeman no more, he stayed squarely on the ground, walked low streets, but of course he thought only of what lay above, of a love on a high-up balcony. He found he no longer knew how to live beside other men, he was used to looking down on treetops, not up, and everywhere he turned he thought he saw her.

Eventually, Adel's father, who had taken away his son's first job without asking, also without asking found Adel another one. He enrolled his son in pilot school, and now Adel flies airplanes that carry mail.

In the end, this is a job he likes very much. He soars above the city, strapped with millions of words on thin pieces of paper. He no longer writes himself (after Nisrine, he has found he cannot) but he likes to handle other people's letters.

Anyway, he says his own decision to stop writing came not from death, but from love. He hasn't written a new poem since the day he met Nisrine in our little apartment, in the children's bedroom. He says that day, he learned a new kind of writing, and he hasn't wanted to go back to the old kind, since. I believe, though, that words became hard for him after her—when they became too hard, he gathered them up, and sent them all to me, the contents of a young life in a single box.

The astonishing text was a text of loss, and loss has defined my life, but I still sometimes take refuge in love. I linger among my books, and try to remember happier times, the excitement of small things I took for granted: Arabic Hair, Adel's blond wink through the window, Nisrine's hand in mine. I am comforted by the fact that she knew great loves in her life, before she left it; that she was able to grow her heart—by her example, I grew mine.

And I cannot help but be glad, too, that, though Qais and Leila met only in heaven, Nisrine and Adel did steal one precious after-noon (the one when we were locked in) on earth.

Let us return to that day. It is the day, Adel says, he found a new kind of writing.

He had just crossed our balcony's threshhold; they had just reunited up close, and run to the bedroom. I sat in the kitchen try-ing not to listen. Nevertheless, now, years later, I enter. Adel's let-ters lie here before me, allowing me to.

The bedroom was small, with a bunk bed, child-sized pencils, her mat on the floor. Among these objects, Adel stood for the first time, all alone, and faced the woman he loved.

Imagine, if you will, this first time, how important it feels. Put yourself in Adel's place—you swung on a rope and knocked in a door to get to her; you want to do well for her, to use this time well. But so far in your life, you've loved only three ways: with words, gestures, and poems. You have never touched.

Just the other day, you made your first foray into fighting for her.

Now, before you stretch a few short hours. And Nisrine, like a new world.

You hold out your hand, shyly. She takes it. This alone sends shivers down your spine.

Once long ago, Adel dreamed of Nisrine, and in the dream she was imperfect and wore a red sari.

Now, in the children's bedroom, the first discovery Adel made was that Nisrine really did have many of the imperfections he'd once dreamed. She had: a sore eye, a bruised toenail. From the birth of her son, he found white lines like lace across her hips and breasts; when he kissed these, they gave like sand.

And so, in these small ways, she proved to him that life can be beautiful as a dream; that a body can live up to what is imagined. He took her in his arms, feeling her soft skin. She opened for him.

Adel was not experienced in love, and he showed his youth. There were only two years between them, but she had lived in another country, borne a child, already married and fallen in love. These experiences gave her knowledge that he had never dreamed of and so, while she quickly led him to a place of full limbs and thick breathing, he ran his hands over her belly, unsure how to proceed. She touched his thigh, and the world gave up in him. He wanted to make her feel that. He traced the map of lines on her breasts, and with every moment his chest grew tighter until he thought he might cry out, but she still hadn't. He stopped, stepped back.

"Nisrine, teach me."

She was also new—not to touch, but to him. She had just spent hours in a room locked up, something she could not submit to again (though, she would). She shook her head, watched for birds out the window.

"It's all right. I'm just glad to be with you."

And she was, but he wanted more than that. He wanted to make her forget this room, these small pencils, to make her feel for a moment what he felt, free.

"No, I want to learn."

"You do?"

He nodded.

He would soon write his last poem: *In Love and Feeling, she is the best teacher.*

And so she rose up, his teacher, her hair loosed like smoke. A long time ago, he had taught her to write Arabic, watched while she leaned over in concentration and traced his letter, *ayn.*

Now, she took his hands in hers; it was her turn to watch over him, guide him the way he had once guided her. And out of their effort together came a new kind of writing. Their hands clasped, he felt curves like soft letters; she led him along them.

Adel thought, Making love is just like a poem.

The sweet flow of words, like water.

He thought, In love, I want to be a great scholar.

So, he sluffed off her hands—now he had learned, he wanted to practice. Just as the great scholars, with soft insistence he studied these new letters, wrote and rewrote them over and over until finally she cried out, one sweet sound like a perfect word.

So, words can be a form of love. They can be felt.

WHEN I THINK BACK ON NISRINE, I don't remember everything she said, but I remember *her*. She is as vivid to me as the sky at sunset, all red-gold, pulsing; or, as the most beautiful book. She touches every part of me, still.

For Adel, it is the same. When he talks of her now, he rarely talks of her notes, but rather, a feeling—one glimpse of a dark hip, the way it lay on his palm like a love knot, the hard center of the world.

He will never forget that hip, how can he? It is seared in his memory, through his eyes, across his lips, a language of love and missing he will always return to, always seek to understand.

ACKNOWLEDGMENTS

My deepest debt is to the residents of Damascus, who shared their city with me, and who taught me it is possible to love a language and a city, even when it is not your own. My heart is with them, and Syria.

Thank you to the Mussareh family and the Jabri family, for making a home for me, and sticking with me all these years. Thank you to wonderful teachers Isam Eidoo, Barbara Romaine, Farha Ghannam, and Tariq Al-Jamil, and to Steven Piker, who first suggested an anthropology student could, if she wanted, also be a writer.

Thank you to Swarthmore College and the Fulbright Program for sending me abroad in the first place, and to Maya Kadmani and her family, Nada Mubarat and her family, Eyad Houssami, Shayna Silverstein, Stephanie Hartgrove, and Katherine Sydenham, for support and dear friendship in Syria during research.

On the writing end: My agent, Cynthia Cannell, wisely and patiently shepherded me through the process of revising and publishing this book.

My editor, Sarah McGrath, first imagined what this book could be; her edits opened up its world and made it, and me, so much richer. Thank you to Riverhead, for publishing so many books I love! And to all those who worked on this book, especially Claire McGinnis and Al Guillen, two amazing publicists; Danya Kukafka, who provided thoughtful edits; Amy Ryan; Claire Sullivan; and Helen Yentus and her team for a beautiful design.

Washington University in St. Louis provided a vibrant community of writers, many of whom commented on early sections of this book. I am indebted to all of them, especially Marshall Klimasewiski for his encouragement, and Kathryn Davis for reading so many drafts! Thank you to Katya Apekina, Anton DiSclafani, and Zachary Lazar. Thank you to Larry Ypil, for a conversation about community and home that made its way into this book.

For time, space, and community, thank you, too, to the Ragdale Foundation, Maumau, the Hambidge Center for Creative Arts and Sciences, and the Vermont Studio Center; also, thank you to the Chicago Department of Cultural Affairs & Special Events, and the Illinois Arts Council for a grant that got me there.

There might not be a book without Sri Pakuwati, Nasria, and Noor, and certainly without them, I would be a different person. Dr. Ahmed Khader has been a true friend for many years; his poetry inspired much of my poetry. The poetic lines on pages 91-92 are a loose translation of an Arabic dedication that he wrote.

My parents gave me the courage to write, and my cousin Rachel led me to study Arabic. I am lucky to have the kind of family that grows together; in adulthood, like in childhood, my parents, along with my aunts and uncles, remain my best examples. I am grateful to them for this, and so much else.

Finally, thank you to my husband, Arthur: first reader, true partner, for sharing this life.